DEC 2 1987

SCARS

SCARS

and other distinguishing marks

Richard Christian Matheson

Illustrated by
Harry O. Morris

Foreword by
Stephen King

Introduction by
Dennis Etchison

SCREAM/PRESS
LOS ANGELES, CALIFORNIA
1987

SCARS
and other distinguishing marks.

Printed in the United States of America.

FIRST EDITION
December, 1987.

ISBN 0-910489-15-7

For Mom and Dad.
Beloved friends,
gentle guides.

CONTENTS

Foreword by Stephen King . . . i
Introduction by Dennis Etchison . . . v
THIRD WIND . . . 1
THE GOOD ALWAYS COMES BACK . . . 11
SENTENCES . . . 17
UNKNOWN DRIVES . . . 29
TIMED EXPOSURE . . . 35
OBSOLETE . . . 39
RED . . . 41
BEHOLDER . . . 45
DEAD END . . . 53
COMMUTERS . . . 63
GRADUATION . . . 67
CONVERSATION PIECE . . . 83
ECHOES . . . 91
INCORPORATION . . . 95
HELL . . . 99
BREAK-UP . . . 105
MR. RIGHT . . . 109
CANCELLED . . . 113
MUGGER . . . 123
THE DARK ONES . . . 127
HOLIDAY . . . 129
VAMPIRE . . . 137
INTRUDER . . . 141
DUST . . . 145
GOOSEBUMPS . . . 149
MOBIUS . . . 157
with Richard Matheson:
WHERE THERE'S A WILL . . . 161

ACKNOWLEDGEMENTS

"Third Wind" copyright © 1984 by Richard Christian Matheson. From *Masks*, edited by J.N. Williamson, Maclay and Associates, Inc.

"The Good Always Comes Back" copyright © 1986 by Richard Christian Matheson. From *Twilight Zone* magazine, Vol. 6, No. 1, TZ Publications, Inc.

"Sentences" copyright © 1982 by Richard Christian Matheson. From *Death*, edited by Charles L. Grant, Playboy Paperbacks, Inc.

"Unknown Drives" copyright © 1979 by Richard Christian Matheson. From *Nightmares*, edited by Charles L. Grant, Berkley Publishing, Inc.

"Timed Exposure" copyright © 1987 by Richard Christian Matheson. First publication.

"Obsolete" copyright © 1987 by Richard Christian Matheson. First publication.

"Red" copyright © 1986 by Richard Christian Matheson. From *Night Cry* magazine, Summer '86, No. 6, Montcalm Publishing, Inc.

"Beholder" copyright © 1982 by Richard Christian Matheson. From *Whispers VI*, edited by Stuart David Schiff, Doubleday and Company, Inc.

"Dead End" copyright © 1979 by Richard Christian Matheson. From *Shadows* 2, edited by Charles L. Grant, Doubleday and Company, Inc.

"Commuters" copyright © 1987 by Richard Christian Matheson. First publication.

"Graduation" copyright © 1977 by Richard Christian Matheson. From *Whispers I*, edited by Stuart David Schiff, Doubleday and Company, Inc.

"Conversation Piece" copyright © 1979 by Richard Christian Matheson. From *Whispers II*, edited by Stuart David Schiff, Doubleday and Company, Inc.

"Echoes" copyright © 1986 by Richard Christian Matheson. From *Horror Show* magazine, Winter '86, Vol. 4, No. 1.

"Incorporation" copyright © 1987 by Richard Christian Matheson. First publication.

"Hell" copyright © 1987 by Richard Christian Matheson. First publication. Lyrics to "When The Music's Over" by Jim Morrison, copyright © 1978 by Doors Music, Inc. Used by permission.

"Break-Up" copyright © 1987 by Richard Christian Matheson. First publication.

ILLUSTRATIONS

facing page

Third Wind 1
The Good Always Comes Back 11
Timed Exposure 35
Beholder 45
Conversation Piece 83
Echoes 91
Break-Up 105
Mr. Right 109
Cancelled 113
Mugger 123
Vampire 137
Goosebumps 149
Mobius 157

RICHARD CHRISTIAN MATHESON

FOREWORD

by Stephen King

I think there are two kinds of short stories: those of style and those of narration. The short fiction of Anne Beattie serves as a good example of the former, those of Robert Bloch of the latter. Beattie writes about a way of feeling and perceiving; Bloch simply tells stories.

I prefer stories that are no more than that to stories of style, but that is no more than a matter of taste—I also eat at McDonald's and prefer bowling to tennis. And there are, occasionally, writers who are able to combine both style and story. They are, of course, the best. You get a spectacular view, and you also get to look at it from the back seat of a chauffeur-driven Cadillac.

Flannery O'Connor comes immediately to mind as the best of these; Faulkner did it sometimes, as in "A Rose for Emily" and "Spotted Horses," but more often used the short story as a stylistic vehicle. Fitzgerald combined style and narration later in his career, but only after he started to need the money. He was not fond of tales like "The Baby Party," published in *The Saturday Evening Post*. I think it one of his best short stories (and am not alone), but Fitzgerald himself dismissed it as a "rent-payer."

In the field of fantasy, those writers able to combine story-as-narration with story-as-style are even rarer. First, there are few writers of purely stylistic fiction to start with, because in genre fiction they rarely get published. There are, of course, a few; David Bunch (who has, I think, now ceased to publish), Robert Silverberg, Barry Malzberg, Thomas Disch (whose greatest triumph, at least in my opinion, was a weird piece of short fiction called "Fun with Your New Head"). Most sf/fantasy writers, however, tell straight stories. They may play with cosmic ideas or describe aliens as weird as Lovecraft's storied non-Euclidian angles, but they're stories without much style, for the most part, because that's what the fans want. And, I repeat, there is nothing wrong with fans wanting stories, or with writers being willing to give them.

But there are a few successful combiners of style and story in this field, as well, many of them women: Chelsea Quinn Yarbro, "James Tiptree, Jr.," Ursula LeGuin, Zenna Henderson come to mind... and men like the late Theodore Sturgeon, the early Ray Bradbury, Gregory Benford... and Richard Christian Matheson.

Matheson is remarkable because his stories are not novellas like many of Sturgeon's best, or short stories of traditional length like such Bradbury classics as "Small Assassin" and "The Emissary." They are, instead, short, tightly wrapped, and abrupt. The typical Matheson story is like something shot out of a staple-gun.

It's not unusual for younger writers to gravitate toward stories of the vignette or almost-vignette length, but it is very unusual to find that rare combination of style and narrative substance in such stories. They are much more apt to either be stylistic vehicles (usually sophomoric and boring) or Frederic Brown-style shaggy dog stories (also sophomoric and boring... unless the author just happens to be Frederic Brown... anyone who's read such classic Brown vignettes as "Bugs" knows what I'm talking about) or poorly-jointed things that look like discarded script ideas for the old *Twilight Zone* show.

I could discuss the stories that follow, but that would turn what's supposed to be an introduction into either a blurb or a critical review—and this is not the place for either of those things. It would also spoil the finely tuned balance that the best of them achieve, not in spite of their brevity but because of it.

The stories vary somewhat in execution and effect—a rather too-elegant way of saying that some are better than others. This is to be expected; Richard Christian Matheson is still a young man and still maturing as a writer. But these stories do more than mark him as a writer to watch: they mark him as a writer to enjoy now.

Stephen King
Wilmington, North Carolina

INTRODUCTION

by Dennis Etchison

1.

Once I dreamed a short story. Or rather I saw acted out before me—as I slept—what was already a perfectly-formed story that needed only to be written.

Actually this has happened to me a number of times. In a couple of cases I have "seen" the typewritten pages of an apparently finished manuscript turning before my eyes; in one instance I managed to wake myself in time to jot down words and lines and paragraphs before they faded in the light, and later my notes proved sufficient for me to reconstruct the story, more as an act of memory than of conscious composition. But it does not usually happen that way. Most of these dreamed stories seem to be happening around me, and the part of my mind that is trained to recognize good source material records their practical value as a matter of course....

In this particular instance, I dreamed not only the events but a title. Unfortunately I allowed my rational mind to get in the way of a smooth transition to the typewriter. I did not understand what "The Cakework Jesus" meant then, and I have yet to entirely plumb its depth. It had to do with a baker who kills his wife, cooks her body inside a life-sized pastry replica of Jesus Christ, and then distributes this huge cake piece by piece to his customers on Easter Sunday.

As you might well imagine, I found this dream disturbing. Such is my peculiar turn of mind that I also found it fascinating. After two or three years of thinking about it, I gave up and in a weak moment cheapened it considerably by writing a minor story in the style of EC Comics entitled "Today's Special," about a butcher who has his partner murdered and displays the body parts for sale in his cold case. But because that superficial treatment failed to convey the mystery and power of the dream, I returned to "The Cakework Jesus" again and again. I finally came up with a version entitled "The Dead Line," after encountering an article about medical experiments involving the farming and harvesting of human bodies as a source for organ transplants. A passage from that story begins with these words:

There is a machine outside my door. It eats people, chews them up and spits out only what it can't use. It wants to get me, I know it does, but I'm not going to let it.

The call I have been waiting for will never come....

I tell you these things as a way of approaching the subject of imagery, the mysterious and potent heart of the artistic experience.

2.

Richard Christian Matheson is a young man, but in less than a decade he may already have published more short stories than I have written in a career that spans an embarrassing number of years.

I was introduced to his work in Stuart David Schiff's first *Whispers* anthology. The story was "Graduation," and I admired its grace, originality and accomplished style. Needless to say, I was amazed to learn that it marked his debut. In my life I have been inordinately impressed by a handful of other "first stories"—by Brian Aldiss, Ray Nelson, Vance Aandahl and the senior Richard Matheson, to name a few—and sometimes this has signaled that a major career was in the offing. In the case of Richard Christian Matheson, I was not disappointed.

His story "Red," for example, seems to me to be an instant classic and a kind of minor masterwork that belongs in a special category of absolutely unforgettable vignettes that includes John Coyne's "The Crazy Chinaman," George Clayton Johnson's "Lullabye and Goodnight," Ramsey Campbell's "Heading Home" and a half-dozen remarkable vignettes by Ray Bradbury. I am tempted to describe "Red" further as part of the present discussion but will restrain myself so as not to lessen its immense impact for those who have yet to read it. Suffice it to say that it deals unflinchingly with an all-but-unbearable moment, and that it does so with an economy of language and an avoidance of emotional excess that only serve to heighten the story's final heartbreaking revelation. Whether it was drawn from an event witnessed in reality or from the shadows of nightmare is something that the author may or may not wish to share. But even if he chooses never to reveal the source, the fact remains that it will almost surely haunt *my* dreams for the rest of my days.

Likewise the central images of "Conversation Piece," "Dead End," "Goosebumps," "Where There's A Will" and "Vampire" are so powerful and resonant that they linger after structure and specific language have been forgotten. The last is a tour de force of such breathtaking virtuosity that it became the first story to be selected for inclusion in my anthology *Cutting Edge*—as how could it not be? When you have struggled with material that is only partially conscious for as long as I have, the appeal of another reckless explorer of the inscape is irresistible; it takes one to know one, so to speak, though his demons are not mine and his methods distinctly his own. Indeed, he achieves time and again in a few deft strokes what I have attempted to much less pointed effect in thousands and thousands of words. And, were the roles reversed, I have no doubt that he could have accomplished such an introduction as this in half the space, with a terseness that would leave us all reeling with admiration for his precision and control.

In short, this book contains some of the most exceptional demonstrations of the art of the short-short story that I have come upon in recent years. And though the collection as a whole is an incredibly fast and entertaining read, the images that last are as intense as the key metaphors of dreamed poems, as vivid as the most life-altering sequences from films seen in childhood whose titles are now lost to us but which will live in our memories long after their fragile reels have turned to dust.

3.

There is a machine outside my door....

One more point deserves to be made here.

Richard Christian Matheson is a child of the movie and TV generation, as am I. We probably fell in love with pictures that move at about the same age—for me it happened at ten, when I sat through two showings of *Shane* and decided before the summer's day was over that I wanted nothing so much as to be a motion picture director.

It eats people....

Richard, however, has done more than wish to be a part of that magical and treacherous industry. Still only in his thirties, he has worked for years, primarily as a television writer, authoring hundreds of prime-time hours and laboring as head writer, story editor or producer on more than a dozen weekly series. More recently, he has moved onto writing and producing for the theatrical market, with two "go" scripts at Steven Spielberg's Amblin Productions, a two-picture commitment with United Artists and another multi-picture deal with Walt Disney Productions. This means that for him the monies to be derived from publishing short fiction are hardly a critical part of his income. And yet, in a town where writers are regarded at worst as slave laborers and at best as necessary evils, he has not only survived but prevailed, at the same time excelling as a literary writer of perfect integrity.

It wants to get me, I know it does, but I'm not going to let it.

It should go without saying that I am deeply moved and heartened by his example. It gives me reason to hope that I will not be eaten alive by the machine that is Hollywood, which is where I live and work from time to time as part of my perversely unshakable dream of contributing to an art form I love with all my heart.

The call I have been waiting for will never come, the protagonist of "The Dead Line" thinks to himself shortly before the end, before he makes his escape into morally-defensible territory, knowing that he may very well be destroyed—if not by the machine then by the rigors of his ethical position....

Richard Christian Matheson is living evidence that neither fate is inevitable, that the word itself may indeed be made flesh. Which is and always should have been encouragement, inspiration and nourishment enough, after all.

Dennis Etchison
Los Angeles, California

SCARS

and other distinguishing marks

Richard Christian Matheson

Illustrated by
Harry O. Morris

"Scars are the record."

THIRD WIND

ANDY CHUGGED UP THE INCLINE, sweatsuit shadowed with perspiration. His Nikes compressed on the asphalt and the sound of his inhalation was the only noise on the country road.

He glanced at his waist-clipped odometer: Twenty-five point seven. Not bad. But he could do better.

Had to.

He'd worked hard doing his twenty miles a day for the last two years and knew he was ready to break fifty. His body was up to it, the muscles taut and strong. They'd be going through a lot of changes over the next twenty-five miles. His breathing was loose; comfortable. Just the way he liked it.

Easy. But the strength was there.

There was something quietly spiritual about all this, he told himself. Maybe it was the sublime monotony of stretching every muscle and feeling it constrict. Or it could be feeling his legs telescope out and draw his body forward. Perhaps even the humid expansion of his chest as his lungs bloated with air.

But none of that was really the answer.

It was the competing against himself.

Beating his own distance, his own limits. Running was the time he felt most alive. He knew that as surely as he'd ever known anything.

He loved the ache that shrouded his torso and even waited for the moment, a few minutes into the run, when a dull voltage would climb his body to his brain like a vine, reviving him. It transported him, taking his mind to another place, very deep within. Like prayer.

He was almost to the crest of the hill.

So far, everything was feeling good. He shagged off some tightness in his shoulders, clenching his fists and punching at the air. The October chill turned to pink steam in his chest making his body tingle as if a microscopic cloud of needles were passing through, from front to back, leaving pin-prick holes.

He shivered. The crest of the hill was just ahead. And on the down side was a new part of his personal route: a dirt road, carpeted with leaves, which wound through a silent forest at the peak of these mountains.

As he broke the crest, he picked up speed, angling downhill toward the dirt road. His Nikes flexed against the gravel, slipping a little.

It had taken much time to prepare for this. Months of meticulous care of his body. Vitamins. Dieting. The endless training and clocking. Commitment to the body machine. It was as critical as the commitment to the goal itself.

Fifty miles.

As he picked up momentum, jogging easily downhill, the mathematical breakdown of that figure filled his head with tumbling digits. Zeroes unglued from his thought tissues and linked with cardinal numbers to form combinations which added to fifty. It was suddenly all he could think about. Twenty-five plus twenty-five. Five times ten. Forty-nine plus one. Shit. It was driving him crazy. One hundred minus—

The dirt road.

He noticed the air cooling. The big trees that shaded the forest road were lowering the temperature. Night was close. Another hour. Thirty minutes plus thirty. This math thing was getting irritating. Andy tried to remember some of his favorite Beatle songs as he gently padded through the dense forest.

Eight Days A Week. Great song. Weird damn title but who cared? If John and Paul said a week had eight days, everybody else just added a day and said...yeah, cool. Actually, maybe it wasn't their fault to begin with. Maybe George was supposed to bring a calendar to the recording session and forgot. He was always the spacey one. Should've had Ringo do it, thought Andy. Ringo you could count on. Guys with gonzo noses always compensated by being dependable.

Andy continued to run at a comfortable pace over the powdery dirt. Every few steps he could hear a leaf or small branch break under his shoes. What was that old thing? Something like, don't ever move even a small rock when you're at the beach or in the mountains. It upsets the critical balances. Nature can't ever be right again if you do. The repercussions can start wars if you extrapolate it out far enough.

Didn't ever really make much sense to him. His brother Eric had always told him these things and he should have known better than to listen. Eric was a self-appointed fount of advice on how to keep the cosmos in alignment. But he always got "D"s on his cards in high school unlike Andy's "A"s and maybe he didn't really know all that much after all.

Andy's foot suddenly caught on a rock and he fell forward. On the ground, the dirt coated his face and lips and a spoonful got into his mouth. He also scraped his knee; a little blood. It was one of those lousy scrapes that claws a layer off and stings like it's a lot worse.

He was up again in a second and heading down the road, slightly disgusted with himself. He knew better than to lose his footing. He was too good an athlete for that.

His mouth was getting dry and he worked up some saliva by rubbing his tongue against the roof of his mouth. Strange how he never got hungry on these marathons of his. The body just seemed to live off itself for the period of time it took. Next day he usually put away a supermarket but in running all appetite faded. The body fed itself. It was weird.

The other funny thing was the way he couldn't imagine himself ever walking again. It became automatic to run. Everything went by so much faster. When he did stop, to walk, it was like being a snail. Everything just... took... so... damn... looooonnnngggg.

The sun was nearly gone now. Fewer and fewer animals. Their sounds faded all around. Birds stopped singing. The frenetic scrambling of squirrels halted as they prepared to bed down for the night. Far below, at the foot of these mountains, the ocean was turning to ink. The sun was lowering and the sea rose to meet it like a dark blue comforter.

Ahead, Andy could see an approaching corner.

How long had he been moving through the forest path? Fifteen minutes? Was it possible he'd gone the ten or so mile length of the path already?

That was one of the insane anomalies of running these marathons of his. Time got all out of whack. He'd think he was running ten miles and find he'd actually covered considerably more ground. Sometimes as much as double his estimate. He couldn't ever figure that one out. But it always happened and he always just sort of anticipated it.

Welcome to the time warp, Jack.

He checked his odometer: Twenty-nine point eight.

Half there and some loose change.

The dirt path would be coming to an end in a few hundred yards. Then it was straight along the highway which ran atop the ridge of this mountain far above the Malibu coastline. The highway was bordered with towering streetlamps which lit the way like some forgotten runway for ancient astronauts. They stared down from fifty-foot poles and bleached the asphalt and roadside.

The path had ended now and he was on the deserted mountain-top road with its broken center line that stretched to forever. As Andy wiped his glistening face with a sleeve, he heard someone hitting a crystal glass with tiny mallets, far away. It wasn't a pinging sound. More like a high-pitched thud that was chain reacting. He looked up and saw insects of the night swarming dementedly around a klieg's glow. Hundreds of them in hypnotic self-destruction dive-bombed again and again at the huge bulb.

Eerie seeing that kind of thing way the hell out here. But nice country to run in just the same. Gentle hills. The distant sea, far below. Nothing but heavy silence. Nobody ever drove this road anymore. It was as deserted as any Andy could remember. The perfect place to run.

What could be better? The smell was clean and healthy, the air sweet. Great decision building his house up here last year. This was definitely the place to live. Pastureland is what his father used to call this kind of country when Andy was growing up in Wisconsin.

He laughed. Glad to be out of *that* place. People never did anything with their lives. Born there, schooled there, married there and died there was the usual, banal legacy. They all missed out on life. Missed out on new ideas and ambitions. The doctor slapped them and from that point on their lives just curled up like dead spiders.

It was just as well.

How many of them could take the heat of competition in Los Angeles? Especially a job like Andy's? None of the old friends he'd gladly left behind in his home town would ever have a chance going up against a guy like himself. He was going to be the head of his law firm in a few more years. Most of those yokels back home couldn't even *spell* success much less achieve it.

But to each his own. Regardless of how pointless some lives really were. But *he* was going to be the head of his own firm and wouldn't even be thirty-five by the time it happened.

Okay, yeah, they were all married and had their families worked out. But what a fucking bore. Last thing Andy needed right now was that noose around his neck. Maybe the family guys figured they had something valuable. But for Andy it was a waste of time. Only thing a wife and kids would do is drag him down; hold him back. Priorities. First things first. *Career.* Then everything else. But put that relationship stuff off until last.

Besides, with all the inevitable success coming his way, meeting ladies would be a cinch. And hell, anyone could have a kid. Just nature. No big thing.

But success. That was something else, again. Took a very special animal to grab onto that golden ring and never let go. Families were for losers when a guy was really climbing. And he, of all the people he'd ever known, was definitely climbing.

Running had helped get him in the right frame of mind to do it. With each mileage barrier he broke, he was able to break greater barriers in life itself, especially his career. It made him more mentally fit to compete when he ran. It strengthened his will; his inner discipline.

Everything felt right when he was running regularly. And it wasn't just the meditative effect; not at all. He knew what it gave him was an *edge*. An edge on his fellow attorneys at the firm and an edge on life.

It was unthinkable to him how the other guys at the firm didn't take advantage of it. Getting ahead was what it was all about. A guy didn't make it in L.A. or anywhere else in the world unless he kept one step ahead of the competition. Keep moving and never let anything stand in the way or slow you down. That was the magic.

And Andy knew the first place to start that trend was with himself.

He got a chill. Thinking this way always made him feel special. Like he had the formula; the secret. Contemplating success was a very intoxicating thing. And with his running now approaching the two and a half-hour mark, hyperventilation was heightening the effect.

He glanced at his odometer: Forty-three point six.

He was feeling like a champion. His calves were burning a little and his back was a bit tender but at this rate, with his breathing effortless and body strong, he could do sixty. But fifty was the goal. After that he had to go back and get his briefs in order for tomorrow's meeting. Had to get some sleep. Keep the machine in good shape and you rise to the top. None of that smoking or drinking or whatever else those morons were messing with out there. Stuff like that was for losers.

He opened his mouth a little wider to catch more air. The night had gone to a deep black and all he could hear now was the adhesive squishing of his Nikes. Overhead, the hanging branches of pepper trees canopied the desolate road and cut the moonlight into a million beams.

The odometer: forty-six point two. His head was feeling hot but running at night always made that easier. The breezes would swathe like cool silk, blowing his hair back and combing through his scalp. Then, he'd hit a hot pocket, that hovered above the road and his hair would flop downward, the feeling of heat returning like a blanket. He coughed and spit.

Almost there.

He was suddenly hit by a stray drop of moisture, then another. A drizzle began. Great. Just what he didn't need. Okay, it wasn't raining hard; just that misty stuff that atomizes over you like a lawn sprinkler shifted by a light wind. Still, it would have been nice to finish the fifty dry.

The road was going into a left hairpin now and Andy leaned into it, Nikes gripping octopus-tight. Ahead, as the curve broke, the road went straight, as far as the eye could see. Just a two lane blacktop laying in state across these mountains. Now that it was wet, the surface went mirror shiny, like a ribbon on the side of tuxedo pants. Far below, the sea reflected a fuzzy moon, and fog began to ease up the mountainside, coming closer toward the road.

Andy checked the odometer, rubbing his hands together for warmth. Forty-nine point eight. Almost there and other than being a little cold, he was feeling like a million bucks. He punched happily at the air and cleared his throat. God, he was feeling great! Tomorrow, at the office, was going to be a victory from start to finish.

He could feel himself smiling, his face hot against the vaporing rain. His jogging suit was soaked with sweat and drizzle made him shiver as it touched his skin. He breathed in gulps of the chilled air and as it left his mouth it turned white, puffing loosely away. His eyes were stinging from the cold and he closed them, continuing to run, the effect of total blackness fascinating him.

Another stride. Another.

He opened his eyes and rubbed them with red fingers. All around, the fog breathed closer, snaking between the limbs of trees and creeping silently across the asphalt. The overhead lights made it glow like a wall of colorless neon.

The odometer.

Another hundred feet and he had it!

The strides came in a smooth flow, like a turning wheel. He spread his fingers wide and shook some of the excess energy that was concentrating and making him feel buzzy. It took the edge off but he still felt as though he were zapped on a hundred cups of coffee. He ran faster, his arms like swinging scythes, tugging him forward.

Twenty more steps.

Ten plus ten. Five times...Christ, the math thing was back. He started laughing out loud as he went puffing down the road, sweat pants drooping.

The sky was suddenly zippered open by lightning and Andy gasped. In an instant, blackness turned to hot white and there was that visual echo of the light as it trembled in the distance, then fluttered off like a dying bulb.

Andy checked his odometer.

Five more feet! He counted it: Five/breath/four/breath/three/breath/two/one and there it was yelling and singing and patting him on the back and tossing streamers!

Fifty miles! Fifty goddamn miles!

It was fucking incredible! To know he could really, actually do it suddenly hit him and he began laughing.

Okay, now to get that incredible sensation of almost standing still while walking it off. Have to keep those muscles warm. If not he'd get a chill and cramps and feel like someone was going over his calves with a carpet knife.

Hot breath gushed visibly from his mouth. The rain was coming faster in a diagonal descent, back-lit by lightning and the fog bundled tighter. Andy took three or four deep breaths and began to slow. It was incredible to have this feeling of edge. The sense of being on *top* of everything. It was an awareness he could surpass limitations. Make breakthroughs. It was what separated the winners from the losers when taken right down to a basic level. The winners knew how much harder they could push to go farther. Break those patterns. Create new levels of ability and confidence.

Win.

He tried again to slow down. His legs weren't slowing to a walk yet and he sent the message down again. He smiled. Run too far and the body just doesn't want to stop.

The legs continued to pull him forward. Rain was drenching down from the sky and Andy was soaked to the bone. Hair strung over his eyes and mouth and he coughed to get out what he could as it needled coldly into his face.

"Slow down," he told his legs. "Stop, goddammit!"

But his feet continued on, splashing through puddles which laked here and there along the foggy road.

Andy began to breathe harder, unable to get the air he needed. It was too wet; half air, half water. Suddenly, more lightning scribbled across the thundering clouds and Andy reached to stop one leg.

It did no good. He kept running, even faster, pounding harder against the wet pavement. He could feel the bottoms of his Nikes getting wet, starting to wear through. He'd worn the old ones; they were the most comfortable.

Jesus-fucking-God, he really couldn't stop.

The wetness got colder on his cramping feet. He tried to fall but kept running. Terrified, he began to cough fitfully, his legs continuing forward, racing over the pavement.

His throat was raw from the cold and his muscles ached. He was starting to feel like his body had been beaten with hammers.

There was no point trying to stop. He knew that, now. He'd trained too long. Too precisely.

It had been his single obsession.

And as he continued to pound against the fog-shrouded pavement all he could hear was a cold, lonely night.

Until the sound of his own screams began to echo through the mountains and fade across the endless road.

THE GOOD ALWAYS COMES BACK

PASSENGERS SNORED as the huddled figure crossed before the headlights. No more than fifteen, she carried an overnight case and apologized as she boarded the Greyhound and bumped passengers along the aisle. Toward the rear, she found a free seat beside a man. She cleared her throat and he glanced up momentarily, then returned his drowsy stare out the window.

"Help yourself," he said.

She smiled and slid the Samsonite under the seat. The driver yawned and steered the huge bus back onto the deserted highway. It was past midnight and the sand to either side of the lonely road stretched to both horizons. As the bus streaked on, bent silhouettes of cacti sprouted here and there like creatures buried alive, and left to die.

"Pretty time of night," she said, snuggling into the seat, leaning it back. "Going all the way?" She wanted to talk.

"Next stop," he mumbled, night shadows smudging his face.

She drew a deep breath and rattled fingernails against her front teeth. He said nothing, listening to the winds that grabbed the bus, squeezing its metal and glass. He lit a cigarette and in the dark, a single spot of orange came and went. Smoke drifted from his tired mouth and he noticed her watching him.

"You know what that reminds me of? It reminds me of this girl that my brother used to go out with."

He said nothing, then realized there was no escape. "She smoked?"

"God...like a chimney. And what happened to her was incredibly gross."

He stared out the window, his reflection bending as the glass was pressed by wind.

"Late at night always reminds me of her, too. She must have been an insomniac or something...she was always calling him at these weird hours."

His eyes were half shut.

"You know what happened to her?" There was no answer but the girl continued, assuming he'd want to know. "...She died. But not of cancer or anything...you know, tobacco-related."

She sighed and squirmed a little in the seat like a restless child. "It was this sore throat she had." She rattled her nails on her teeth again. "She just felt a tickling in her throat one morning and then...zap, right into the hospital."

The driver was fighting headwinds and the bus creaked.

"Sore throat?"

The girl nodded, removed a Kleenex from her sweater pocket and dabbed at slightly reddened nostrils. "She couldn't breathe right or something. Gives me the creeps thinking about it." She closed her eyes tightly and opened them. "I really liked her, too."

The man sucked on his cigarette, saying nothing.

"And here's the worst part, if you want to know the whole story..."

He looked at her, unexpected curiosity perching on his features. "Sure," he heard himself say, not knowing quite why.

She hesitated. "Oh, I don't want to bother you with this. Let's just enjoy the ride."

He sensed her need to talk and his expression didn't stop her.

She looked at him vulnerably. "Well, my brother died a couple weeks later. It was a car accident. But I have my own theory. See, I think he was so depressed about his girlfriend that he wasn't paying attention... I doubt he even knew what hit him."

The man noticed the corners of her mouth twitch, her glance fall. "Were you close?" He was in too deep to turn back.

She nodded, slowly, sadly. "Very. I know brothers and sisters always love each other, but we had something special. He was very likeable." She brightened. "Did you come from a big family?"

He didn't respond for a moment. Then came a whispered answer. "Only child."

He was exhausted and leaned his head against the window, trying to doze off. She watched him.

"You know," she said, almost immediately, causing him to shake awake, "I really shouldn't pick at my nose like this." She smiled a charming, little girl smile. "There's tons of nerves that are very sensitive. You can paralyze your face."

As the bus swayed, the driver's tired eyes crept upward to the visor rearview; bloodshot, blinking dully. He shifted his shoulders.

"Never heard that," the man said, trying to tune her out.

She pulled at the elasticized pouch on the seat before her and nodded seriously.

"Most people haven't. But my aunt had it happen." She gestured to her face. "Can't even smile anymore. Imagine not being able to smile."

The man looked over and the girl was blinking sadly at him. Outside a highway patrol car wailed by, sirens and lights carving the way. Then it was gone. Taking a deep breath, the man pushed his feet against the floorboard and slid up in his seat. He wanted to change seats and his eyes searched the bus. But there were no other seats and he decided to change the subject; she wasn't going to let him sleep.

"Where you headed?" He rearranged his hair, which had been flattened by the window.

"New Mexico. My dad's sending me to a private school out there. Hollister? Heard of it?"

He hadn't. She wrinkled up her nose, collapsing the spray of freckles.

"It's supposed to be real nice...horses, private rooms." She shrugged. "I'll miss my dog, though."

He crushed out his cigarette. "What kind of dog?"

She pulled a photo from her purse of a pretty young girl wrestling with a golden retriever.

"That's him. And me." The man took the picture and held it. He pointed to a woman standing in the photo's background. "Who's that?"

She crisscrossed the fingers of both hands into a delicate weave. "My mom. She's been pretty sick. That's why I'm going to Hollister. Dad figured the pressure of being around her would be too much for me." She smiled, weakly. "The doctors say her chances aren't...very good."

The man felt bad for her and offered some gum.

"Pretty rough year," he said, as they both chewed.

Her eyes began to water. "It's been horrible. But my dad says these things run in cycles. The good will come back. That's what he always says. But I don't know. To be absolutely honest with you, I'm real scared. Seems like my whole life is falling apart."

The man thought about that and looked at her, hearing her pain and fear. "I think your dad is right. The good never does stay away too long."

She looked at him, wanting to believe every word as the bus hummed trance sounds.

"I just love my mom so much," she said, embarrassed to self-consciousness by her tears. "I mean, most of the girls I know just barely tolerate their parents. But for me..."

She began to cry and the man had to do something. "It sounds like you're really close."

"Mothers and daughters should like each other. I guess I feel more that way toward her than my dad, even though he's okay, too. It's just I sort of idolize her." She suddenly seemed awkward with this candor. "Is that sick?"

The man gave the girl's arm a squeeze and the two rocked as the bus leaned off the highway and slowed into a small town. A ghostly terminal was ahead and inside, white neon sizzled. Newspapers scratched over cement, benches sat empty. There was no traffic.

"Briston," announced the driver, as he braked to a stop before the terminal, yawned and poured thermos coffee. Outside, wind rose, sounding like a woman moaning over a dead child.

"My stop," said the man.

"Looks lonely out there," she said.

They both peered through the dirty window and allowed a personal moment to come and pass. Then, he nodded and slid past her legs, grabbing a duffel from the overhead rack.

"Thanks for listening," she said. "Sorry I talked your ear off. Guess I've got insomnia like my brother's girlfriend or something..."

He winked. "Good for watching old movies on TV." His smile was warm. "Hey...good luck, huh?"

They looked at each other, and she grasped his hand. "The good always comes back, right?" Her eyes were weak and frightened, like she'd come a very long way.

He nodded. "Yeah. It always does. Have fun at school."

With that, he headed past the other sleeping passengers and out the door. Outside, the wind reached beneath his clothes and he hoisted his duffel, walking toward the deserted terminal, across the street. Suddenly, a voice called from behind and he turned to see her smiling face, chin resting on the window she'd lowered. He waved at her and over the sound of the bus rumbling out, she yelled to him.

"Hey, what's your name, anyway?"

"What's yours?" he yelled back, grinning.

"It's a secret," she screamed, waving at him as the bus began to pull away. Its engines drowned her out as she yelled one last thing he couldn't make out.

"What?" he screamed, standing in the middle of the deserted town's main street.

"I said I really like you!" She was cupping hands to her mouth and grinning.

Greasy exhaust washed over him as he stood there and smiled, watching the bus sway into the night and saw her run to the rear window. Her face filled it and she giggled delightedly, waving and growing smaller as the taillights tinted her features red. He chuckled and waved back, trying to yell goodbye. But he never got the word out.

He just stood there, feeling his throat grow raw, realizing from the moment she'd sat down, he'd never had a chance.

SENTENCES

HARRY FIRST NOTICED the advertisement as he rode on the subway. The ad made him straighten and take notice and he draped the paper in his lap, running his finger across the print.

> *Do you want to know what's really wrong with your life?* WE HAVE THE ANSWER! *If you are tired of:* drugs, sex, religion, T.M., EST, psychoanalysis, etc.... *NO WONDER!! None of these contain the answer! Only we have that. If you want your life to make sense to you, call the following number for a personal consultation.*

To say the least, Harry was jolted. He had been looking for something like this for months. He was, to the point of outrage, fed up with his life and felt it high time he get to the bottom of the shoddy hand he'd been dealt.

Shoving and shouldering his way out of the subway at the next station, he placed a call to the number indicated in the ad, at a glass enclosed phone booth. His call answered, he was calmly assured that the service specified was sincere and completely effective by a cordial secretary. He was also informed of the rate; a flat five hundred dollars.

As convinced as was possible in so short a call, Harry made an appointment to come in the following day, stipulating no commitment. The secretary readily agreed to the terms.

The following afternoon, Harry was sitting in the office of Mr. Lance Webb, one of the agent-counselors for the business which Harry had by now discovered was called *Script Sure*.

Smiling, Webb sat behind his formidable pecan desk regarding Harry.

"Well, I suppose you're here to find out how it all works," he said, "am I right?"

"You are," replied Harry. "But before we get to talking, I'd like to know just how you are able to do what you claim in your ad."

Webb smiled.

"We prefer, of course, to have the payment first," he said, pleasantly stroking a thin moustache.

"But...how can I be sure?" Harry's voice was rich with doubt. "I don't mean to be impolite, but if I lose five hundred bucks on some con-scheme, that'll be the last straw."

"I understand your hesitation, Mr. Addley. However we at *Script Sure* are solidly backed by all of our customers. Some of their letters of accolade hang on the wall behind me."

Webb gestured to several framed letters.

"However, if you prefer declining our services I will respect your wishes and terminate this meeting." Webb was icily polite. "Others are waiting." Harry stared at Webb and the letters and thought for a good minute. He reached into his coat pocket.

"Alright," he said, making out a check. "I'm afraid the fact of the matter is, I really haven't much to lose."

Webb nodded approvingly as he examined the check Harry handed to him and placing it in a desk drawer, leaned forward in his chair.

"I would like to take as little of your time as possible, Mr. Addley. Therefore, to be quite simple and clear," he said matter-of-factly, "your life, in its totality, is a script. That's the answer."

"What?" said Harry, unimpressed.

"A script," repeated Webb.

"I don't follow you," said Harry, squinting with budding frustration. "What is this, Transactional Analysis or something? I've read all that garbage. I thought this was completely different."

Webb laughed.

"No, no, Mr. Addley. You see, this is completely different. The script I referred to is a tangible structure, not just a loose concept. You are living a script. It was written, by a writer, just for you."

Harry stared at Webb, unflinchingly.

"You're crazy," he said.

"Less than you think," said Webb, happily.

Harry eyed him for a moment trying to assemble a response worthy of reason. Instead he slammed his hands down on the armrests of his chair.

"Oh, good God," he exclaimed, "this is nonsense."

Harry was about to demand his money back but stopped for a moment. An idea was sifting through his mind and his mouth formed a stringent, knowing smile. He could beat Webb at his own game.

"Well," began Harry, "if what you say is true, Mr. Webb, then perhaps you might have some idea as to how I could get my script changed."

"Do you mean rewritten?" asked Webb, candidly.

"Exactly," said Harry, his effective entrapment causing him to gloat as he crossed his arms.

Webb didn't bat an eye.

"That would naturally require an additional expenditure," he said, smoothly. "Another two thousand, to be exact. But if you are definitely interested..."

Harry, surprised as he found himself by this reply, of course, was. Still much confused, he wrote down an address Webb read to him from a little black book and after suspiciously shaking Webb's hand, left.

As he rode through the city in a dingy cab, Harry thought about the notion of his life being a script. He didn't believe it. But on the off chance that what Webb said was true, Harry knew one thing. His script was no comedy. It was more like a sordid, low-budget melodrama. Harry's script would definitely not have made a movie you could take your family to.

The driver pulled to the curb and Harry got out and paid him. The cabbie roared away and Harry looked up at the sign on the store front. It read, 229 S. Maple—ABE'S KOSHER DELI. Harry shook his head incredulously and walked toward the door.

As he opened the door, he was met inside by a gust of chilly air-conditioning and the rich scent of cold cuts.

He approached the front display counter and leaned over it. There was a butcher standing with his back to Harry, behind the counter. Harry discerned that it was likely Abe, himself.

"Excuse me," said Harry.

"Yeah, what'll it be?" asked the man, turning to face Harry, bloody cleaver in hand. He had a thick paunch and wiped his free hand of animal innards, smearing them on his starched apron.

"I was sent over here by Mr. Webb at *Script Sure*," said Harry.

"Oh, yeah, yeah," grunted the man, "you're looking for Eddie. He's upstairs. Office is the last one on the right," he gestured toward the upstairs area with his cleaver.

"Thank you," said Harry, his suspicions of a clumsy con renewed.

"And tell him we're out of sliced almonds for his ice cream, will you?" added the corpulent butcher.

"Sure," said Harry, heading for the stairs, "why not?"

Once upstairs, he easily found the office. As he stood outside its door, he could faintly hear the cadence of a muted typewriter clacking inside. As he knocked, he noticed that hand-painted on the glass pane insert was the name, EDWARD OMNEY.

"Come in!" yelled a voice from inside the office. "It's open!"

Harry hinged open the door and walked in.

Inside he was met by a minuscule office virtually immobilized by disorder. The floor, cheaply carpeted, was covered almost from wall to wall with notebook binders of differing colors. The binders also covered the battered desk in the right center of the tiny office, barely leaving room for the worn typewriter.

On one of two chairs before the desk sat a humming blade fan, tossing three ribbons tied to its front. The walls were a chipped caramel patina, coats of nicotine thin on their surface. Behind the desk, seated on a squeaking chair, was a tiny, harried-looking Jewish man about fifty. He was nearly bald and resembled a scaled down Ritz brother with a manner suggesting the patience of a lit stick of dynamite.

"Hi ya," welcomed the man, with a teeter-totter Yiddish accent, "what's the good word?"

"Good afternoon," said Harry, "are you Eddie?"

"Last time I checked," said Eddie, dropping a heaping spoonful of bromo-seltzer into a glass of water. "You like vanilla ice cream?" he asked, as he stirred the frothing drink with his finger.

"Because if you do," he continued, "I'm stuffed and there's a whole dish in my little fridge, there." He pointed over to the corner.

"No thank you," said Harry, his appetite poor since the onset of his problems, "I haven't been eating well lately."

"Sorry to hear that," said Eddie, "you ought to get a hobby. Myself, I do sit-ups. Lots of sit-ups. And look at me, I'm fit as a fiddle." He patted his stomach hard with his palm then leaned back in his chair and gulped down his fizzing seltzer.

"By the way, the butcher downstairs says he's out of nuts for your ice cream," said Harry, as he watched Eddie finish the glass.

"It's just as well," said Eddie, wiping foam from his lips, "they give me indigestion; can't write with indigestion. Listen, you sure you don't want some ice cream?"

"No," said Harry, ready to get down to business. "Look, Eddie, I'll get directly to the point. I was sent here by *Script Sure*. I'm very unhappy with my script and I want it rewritten."

"Naturally," said Eddie, "everybody's a writer. What's the matter with it?" he asked, muffling several burps brought on by the bromo.

"What *isn't* the matter with it," said Harry. "My life is a disaster. Every day is more horrible than the one before it."

"Oh, yeah?" said Eddie, beginning to get interested.

"How could you do this to me?" asked Harry, miserably. "My

wife left me for a trumpet player, my boss laid me off last week, my kid is on pills and I think I'm getting an ingrown toenail."

"Right!" yelled Eddie. "Now I remember. That was a good one. Knocked the final draft out over a weekend, as I recall."

"How long do you usually take?" asked Harry, deeply upset at having the approximate importance of a thrown-together high school book report.

"A week or two," said Eddie, "give or take..."

"And you did mine in a weekend?" Harry was beginning to feel more like the Cliff's Notes which inspired the book report.

"Pretty sure I did," said Eddie. "The wife was out of town, seeing her mother, I think." He stared at the ceiling, trying to remember. "Or did I have the flu?"

"Oh, great," said Harry.

"Hey, don't be put off," said Eddie. "I do some of my best work under pressure."

Harry made a displeased face.

"Now what were you saying about wanting it changed?" asked Eddie.

Harry realized that it was definitely in his best interest to find out how the company he was entrusting his future to operated. After all, he wouldn't buy a car without kicking the tires good and hard, once or twice.

"Not so fast," said Harry, "there's a few things I'd like to know first. Like for instance how long people have had scripts."

"Long time," replied Eddie, "since the beginning I would expect."

"Don't you know?" asked Harry.

"No," said Eddie, lighting a cheap cigar, "not really. I just started on here a while ago."

Harry was having a hard time absorbing this information and felt an ulcerous twitch.

"Well, what did you do before?" he asked.

"Oh, a little of this, a little of that," replied Eddie, "mostly just bummed around. Wrote poetry, taught judo."

Harry visibly cringed at hearing this. There was minimal comfort in the prospect of having his future in the hands of a deadbeat poet who splintered two-by-fours with his feet. Harry wanted more from a rewrite man.

"Look Eddie," said Harry, "I'm not so sure about your credentials. I mean your background sounds pretty shaky to me."

"Big deal," said Eddie, "Lincoln was born in a log cabin. You gonna stand there and tell me Abe Lincoln wasn't a terrific president?"

"Well, no, but..."

"*But* nothing. I rest my case. What's to talk? Tell me what you want and let me get to work." Eddie sounded a bit testy at having had his probity slighted. Harry was getting confused and upset by everything he had heard. He was beginning to hyperventilate.

"Look, Eddie, this is all pretty new to me. I mean I don't understand where this thing with scripts came from. Or whose idea it was for that matter. I don't get it. I just don't understand what the hell is going on." Harry's voice sounded almost crumbly.

"I just never thought it would be like this," he whined, rising from his chair and walking to the window. He looked out onto the busy avenue. "I mean, it's crazy! It's totally crazy!"

"Hey, come on buddy, it's not that bad. Take it easy. Hey, what's your name, anyway? You never told me."

"Don't you know? I thought you knew everything."

"Can't remember them all. I do a lot of scripts."

Harry turned from the window.

"Harry. Harry Addley."

"Right. I remember something like that," said Eddie. "Well, look Harry, I can't remember how I wrote you; are you a religious man?"

"Fairly," said Harry, sniffing to himself, "I respond spiritually to organ music."

"Right," said Eddie. "Well, what I'm getting at here is that, if you are, you might not want to know how this all works. It might shake you up. Things aren't always as they seem."

"For instance," said Harry, "most people don't think of the Lord as a Jewish writer, who works out of a kosher deli."

"Well, I'm only one of the many that *Script Sure* employs but you're getting the idea. See, I didn't do such a bad job. You're pretty quick."

Harry sighed and sitting down pointed the fan at his face; slightly faint.

"Hey! I'm burning up in here, as is," squawked Eddie.

"Why don't you make it snow?" asked Harry.

"You see. There you go again," said Eddie, "that's all just a stereotype. That stuff has all been updated. No more lofty images. Things are more efficient these days. We even advertise to cover office expenses. We run a little in the red. You know, paper clips, coffee cups... it adds up."

"Sure," said Harry, morosely, his mind elsewhere. "And to think I bothered going to Sunday School. I should have prayed for better dialogue and characterization. For that matter, the Bible should have been written by Eugene O'Neill. He probably would have picked up the pace a little."

"Hell of a writer," agreed Eddie.

Harry reflected on his situation and decided to make the best of it.

"Well look, Eddie, when can you get to my script?"

"You got the two G's?" asked Eddie.

"Yeah, I can get it," said Harry. "It's worth it. I mean it's my damn life."

Eddie got a hurt expression on his face.

"Sure it's easy for you to talk about my writing like that. You try writing one of these babies some time. Give you migraines," said Eddie.

"Sorry," said Harry, "you know what I meant."

"It's okay," said Eddie, "I'll live."

"Well, when do you think I could have it?" asked Harry.

"Week and a half. I'll change everything. Believe me, you'll love it."

"I want to be happy, Eddie. I want my wife back. I want a better job with a raise, I want my kid straightened out and I want new feet."

"Same size?" asked Eddie, making some brief notes.

"Maybe a little smaller," offered Harry.

"How about a nine-D?"

"I like it," said Harry.

"Okay," said Eddie, "I'll take it from here. I know exactly what you're after. Listen, Harry, I have a terrific idea. Why don't you take a vacation until I have the script ready. You ski?"

"No," said Harry, "I guess you didn't have time to put that in. Your wife must have come home."

"Aw, come on Harry, don't be nasty. We'll fix everything up for you. I'll throw something together this afternoon for you to go skiing in Aspen, Colorado. How does that sound? Is Eddie looking out for you or isn't he?" Eddie smiled.

Harry looked at him with a critical sigh.

"We'll see."

Four days after his conversation with Eddie, Harry was on the slopes at Aspen. He had never put skis on in his entire life yet he was doing expertly on even the most complicated of maneuvers. He traversed moguls with ease and was even able to slalom down the most difficult slope on a single ski. His ingrown toenail had even miraculously disappeared.

He realized it was all Eddie's doing and no longer questioned his competence as a writer. He wasn't such a bad guy, thought Harry.

He just worked for *Script Sure* because he needed the work. Christ, somebody had to do the job.

That afternoon, after a warm soup and hot chocolate at the Chalet, Harry decided to go for a cross-country ski. He would take some food and head out for the unspoiled flats of Aspen's most spectacular country. There, beneath the towering mountains, he could celebrate the prospect of his new life. He finished his lunch and went to get his equipment.

Hunched over his typewriter, far from the magnificence of the Aspen peaks, sat Eddie, re-working Harry's script. As he worked on the section about the cross-country ski, he decided to really do a special job for Harry to make up for the trouble *Script Sure* had caused him. He decided to really give Harry an exciting run for his two thousand dollars. Florid descriptions began to roll off Eddie's fingertips as he furiously typed scene after scene for Harry's stimulating new revision.

He included a breakneck escape from an avalanche which Harry was to barely avert at the last second. He also included, with much chuckling to himself, an encounter with a beautiful ski bunny for Harry, culminating with Harry and the young lovely making wild love through the night before a large fireplace.

As if this weren't enough, Eddie described Harry's next day as being even more action-filled and death-defying. He was to make a three-hundred-foot ski jump, through mid-air and land perfectly on one ski, then immediately afterward participate in a tequila drinking contest in the Chalet which he would win after successfully downing four bottles of the hot liquor.

The evening of that same day, he would arm-wrestle a Norwegian ski instructor for the instructor's woman and overwhelm the massive Nordic giant after a two-hour sweat-drenched struggle.

Later that evening, having ditched his original ski bunny, he would be made love to by his prize. She would be an indefatigable, sensual Amazon who would take Harry to her private chalet and show him bizarre anatomical innovations that he would theretofore have thought were certainly federal offenses and only have dreamed of. It would be a deeply gratifying evening.

For the following day, Eddie was putting in descriptions of Harry's Porsche race through the ice-covered Aspen roads against the then-reigning champion race driver in all the world. Harry would win by a nerve-wracking hair and come near to death when his turbo-powered racecar would almost skid off a cliff. The former champion would later weep before a gathered crowd and present Harry his trophy, congratulating him for being a brilliant competitor and a gentleman. Before bringing him back, to give him his new job, Eddie included a few more thrills for Harry. Included among these, were the eventual killing of the Norwegian ski instructor, in self-defense, by snipping the cable to his chair lift. He also threw in a new sexy moustache for Harry on a face which had formerly been capable of only sparse peach fuzz.

What a script this was!

Eddie was exultant. This was the best one he had ever done. As he was typing in a description of Harry coolly winning big at the tables in Vegas on his way back from Aspen, his phone rang.

"Hello," said Eddie, still typing, putting the phone in the crook of his shoulder.

"Hello Eddie, this is Jerry."

"Jerry! Great to hear from you. What's up?"

"How about lunch?"

"Have to take a raincheck Jer. Caught up with a rewrite and it's coming out great."

"Oh, come on Eddie. If I can put down my scripts for awhile, you can. Me and some of the guys are going for sandwiches. Larry's coming, so's Sid."

"Jeez, Jer, I'd love to but I really can't."

"They're busy with rewrites, too, Eddie."

"I know. But this script is the best one I've ever done. It might win me the annual *Soul* award from *Script Sure*."

"That good, huh?"

"Better," said Eddie, confidently. "It's brilliant and I'd really rather stay in 'til I'm done with it."

"What's it about?" asked Jerry, a little envious.

"This guy came in a few days ago with a bad script. Same story; we've all heard it a million times; wanted a rewrite. Seems his wife left him, his kid was on pills, got laid off his job. Even had an ingrown toenail."

"Eddie, you're gonna hate me for this, but did the guy's wife leave him for a trumpet player?"

"Yeah, that's right. How'd you know?"

Jerry laughed.

"I worked on that script. Did the first draft, way back. It's a good thing that guy came in to see you. Things were only going to get worse on that script, as I recall."

"What do you mean?" asked Eddie, wondering if something like this would disqualify him from the *Soul* award competition.

"Well, of course with that condition of his..."

Eddie interrupted, suddenly.

"Condition! What condition?"

"Oh, you must have missed it. Yeah, as I remember, I gave him a very weak heart. But don't worry. Just don't give him anything too strenuous in your rewrites," said Jerry, cheerily. "Now how about that lunch?"

Eddie didn't answer. He just leaned back in his chair, face expressionless, and downed another bromo.

UNKNOWN DRIVES

AHEAD, the truck pulled onto the road and cut off Don's Mustang.

"Damn!" said Don.

The truck was going no more than twenty-five miles an hour. Don's wife, Kerry, shook her head in disbelief.

"These local farmers must think they own the road," she began. "The speed limit is fifty-five."

Don looked at the rear of the truck. In faded letters on the wooden cage that surrounded the bed was written something.

"Field's Produce," Don read aloud, "...great, he's probably delivering to the next county."

Kerry smiled.

"Well, there goes the vacation," she said lightly.

"Let's just see," replied Don under his breath.

He leaned his body to the left and gradually pulled the Mustang out into the opposing lane. As he accelerated, he quickly snapped the steering wheel to the right, and the Mustang swerved sharply back into the right lane.

"What's the matter?" asked Kerry, startled.

Don sighed.

"Road work," he explained, pointing to the left side of the road.

At that moment, the Mustang passed a row of hinged yellow

barricades, all crowned with blinking orange lights. The barricades completely blocked off the opposing lane.

Ahead, the truck was still going twenty-five. There was no way for Don to get around it and it went no faster. Just a slow, never-changing, aggravating twenty-five.

Don looked at the other lane. It was still blocked. He edged the Mustang slightly to the left and looked down the road as far as he could see, then pulled back into his lane.

"Those barricades look like they go on for a couple of miles," he said, with controlled frustration. "They're repaving the other lane."

Kerry nodded understanding and patted her husband's leg calmingly. She reached to a styrofoam picnic container on the floor and removed a Coke.

"Sip?" she asked.

"No," said Don, his eyes glued to the truck. "Not now. I want to pass this guy. He's beginning to bug the shit out of me."

Don could see the back of the farmer's head. The man seemed completely at ease. His right hand brought a thinly smoking pipe to his mouth.

Don made an impatient face and honked several times, holding the horn down.

"Pull over, you sonofabitch!" he hissed.

The farmer ignored the honking. He puffed easily on his pipe and the smoke furled in the truck cab.

"That smug bastard," said Don, looking at the Mustang's speedometer incredulously, "I think he's going slower."

Kerry could see Don getting angrier.

"He's just an old man, Don. I'm sure his slow driving is just habit. I didn't notice him slowing down."

"Like hell he didn't," insisted Don. "I could see it on the speedometer."

Kerry tried to take Don's right hand and he pulled away from her nervously. He glanced at her, mood brittle.

"He's hogging the road," said Don, "I've got to get around him. This could go on all day."

He quickly looked to his left.

The yellow barricades had ended. The other lane was open again.

"Finally," said Don.

Without hesitating, he pulled the Mustang out and tried to pass the truck. He was just about ready to floor the engine when his pulse doubled. Both he and Kerry screamed at what was coming as they swayed fully into the opposing lane.

A one-lane bridge was a few yards ahead.

As the truck lethargically rolled across the bridge, Don slammed on his brakes, putting all his weight on the pedal, eyes widening.

The Mustang skidded loudly and almost slid over a muddy embankment into the marsh water beneath the bridge.

There was a last cloud of exhaust as the engine stalled. All was still for a moment.

"Are you all right?" Don asked Kerry in a throaty whisper. He leaned over the steering wheel, breathing heavily.

Kerry looked over at him, shock still on her face.

"I wasn't expecting that," she said, mouth dry.

Don reached over, hugged her.

"I'm beginning to hate this route," said Kerry, reaching to the glove compartment and pulling out a box of Kleenex.

"I'm in no rush, Don," she said, wiping his face, then her own. "Can't we just drive slower..."

"No," said Don, tensely, "this is the only route through the county and I'll be damned if I'm going to let some old man make me late."

"Your brother won't mind if we're a few minutes late," she said. "Please, Don."

He ignored her and put the Mustang in reverse. He pulled free from the muddy embankment and pushed the transmission into DRIVE. He floored the pedal and the Mustang bolted back onto the road.

"I'm going to pass him," said Don. "All I need is a clear stretch."

He looked over at Kerry as they sped along the highway. She was sipping Coke.

"Just let me try a couple more times," he said, reassuringly. "I'll quit if it's no good. I promise."

Kerry looked at him, smiled weakly.

"Good," said Don, coming up behind the truck. "Then let's leave this fucker in the dust and get on with it. We'll show him."

The truck was rocking slightly in front of them. It still didn't waver from twenty-five.

Don watched the truck in fascination.

"He must have something in that rig to keep it going one speed," he said, tapping his fingers on the steering wheel.

In the truck, the farmer was still smoking his pipe. He adjusted his hat as he drove, shrugged his shoulders a bit.

Sensing the time was right to pass, Don pulled the Mustang into the other lane.

It was no good.

A truck was coming from the other direction. Don pulled back into the lane; waited again.

"Almost," he said to Kerry. "Next one."

He edged every few seconds to the left so he could see the oncoming traffic.

"Goddamn this," muttered Don, as several enormous trucks passed on his left.

"Look!" interrupted Kerry.

The truck was braking and signaling for a right-hand turn. It began to curve slowly to the right.

"Patience," said Don with an ironic smile, "that's all it took."

Not missing his chance, he shoved the pedal to the floor with his right foot and the Mustang roared around to the side of the truck. It streaked along the opposing lane and Don gripped the wheel firmly. He began to roll down his window.

"Take that Coke, now," he was smiling at Kerry.

But it was too late.

From the right side of the farmer's truck, off a side road, in Don's blind spot, came another enormous foundry truck. He and

Kerry ran directly into it and were thrust bloodily through the Mustang windshield. Their bodies landed on the road and pools of deep-red blood formed hideous perimeters around them.

The Mustang suddenly caught fire, and explosions of hot metal ransacked the silence of the countryside. Flaming colors of orange, red, and blue were everywhere.

Several pasture animals looked on, chewing and kicking their hooves. The fire began to go out and the Mustang sizzled and groaned on the highway.

The truck pulled up in front of the farmhouse and the farmer got out and knocked his pipe against the muddy running board. Chunks of burned tobacco tumbled out and he walked to the kitchen door.

He entered, and his wife was standing at the stove, stirring a boiling stew. He filled his pipe with new tobacco.

"How was your day?" she asked.

He held a match to his pipe bowl.

"Good day," he said. "I got me one."

TIMED EXPOSURE

THEY MET at this very strange party in Malibu.

The house was Moorish design and a heavy, industry crowd sat on tubby *Road To Morocco* pillows, danced, snorted and lied to each other, as perfect surf supplied a metronome.

She was an actress, studying at one of the local academies and getting in for Equity-waiver auditions. He was ...she wasn't sure. She asked him and he dropped two new cubes into her vodka tonic and said:

"I work when I feel inspired."

They stood by the bar's open glass door, watching the ocean foam, and his white scarf was suddenly stolen by night wind, flying into the blackness; a ghostly serpent. She stared into his dark eyes, and he touched her cheek, asking if she were alone.

An hour later, they walked on the beach, laughing; celebrating having found each other at such a dull party. He was a world traveler named Gregory and she liked his sense of humor, though he preferred not to talk about himself. Still, as they crunched through moist sand, she managed to learn he'd been married, loved dogs, and knew the address of every great restaurant in Paris. She told him she'd never been to Paris.

At nine-thirty sharp, a screening of *The African Queen* began in the plush living room which rose over a mirror tide and she sat beside him, nibbling crackers and sharing funny secrets.

Now and then, during the film, she would peek over at him and he'd smile, making her feel pleasingly like a child; like he watched her as a father might, taking his little girl to her first movie. As Humphrey Bogart's stomach grumbled and Katherine Hepburn glared politely, the two new friends held hands and she looked over, aching to touch him; to feel him.

At midnight, guests began to yawn and sleepy, stoned-out couples hugged the host, saying it was the best party they'd ever been to. He was a tanned studio sultan who kissed their cheeks and smiled, though it was impossible to tell if he believed every word or memorized which faces deceived him.

That was when Gregory asked to drive her home.

She was thrilled, feigned reluctance, and said she couldn't impose. But when he threw an arm around her and whispered a joke in her ear, she laughed and grabbed her purse.

They took his Mercedes 500 SL and streaked down Pacific Coast Highway, listening to the Beatles' *White Album* cranked to a million watts, laughing like insane teenagers. The top was down and their hair was pulled into Dracula tightness by cool winds as the Mercedes purred through fog and he reached over, pulling her closer. Ahead, they could see a fuzzy necklace of lights that stretched down the throat of the coastline, fifty miles south, lighting the way.

"Beautiful," she said, watching the wipers arm-wrestle mist.

He slid his electric window down and wind swirled his hair into a tidepool as they ran a red light and sped south toward her apartment in Brentwood.

That's when they saw it.

A traveling carnival. It was standing in the parking lot of the Malibu Colony Market and their faces were awash in pink and green neon as they drove in and stared at the huge pendulum rockets that had screams pouring from spinning tips.

He killed the engine, did some lines of blow with her and ran warm fingers across her cold face. She touched her lips to his salty palm and gently tasted it, as a cage full of monkeys shrieked in the distance.

"You taste good," she said, words carried from her mouth on visible breath, like a comic-book character whose ideas emerge in a balloon.

They wandered through the sour smells of the carnival, drinking blue slush and watching an elephant with sad eyes stand on one foot. And when they threw ping-pong balls into empty aquariums, he won her a small goldfish which she accepted like it were a diamond. She carried it in a Baggie and it swam and stared at them, dangling in her perfectly manicured hand.

They strolled near a giant Ferris wheel and were drawn by pulsing bulbs that guarded the portal to the COIN ARCADE. Inside, on a lake of sawdust, they had their fortunes told by "Madame Destiny" who stared frozenly, until slipped a token, then came alive, mechanical face tensing with worry. She told them both to beware of strangers, then lifted a Mona Lisa smile and said evil thoughts couldn't be hidden. After more trance sounds, which she hummed ominously, the seer became stiff again, suddenly dead, eyes closing, painted hands lifeless over the chipped crystal ball. They thanked her with amused smiles and walked-on seeing a row of photo booths, ratty curtains half drawn. On each was stenciled: *Four Photos—50 Cents.*

"I have a little more change," he said, sliding fingers into his pants pocket. She said she was game and tapped at her goldfish as its features bulged curiously.

They barely fit inside the booth and she told him it reminded her of an old Marx Brothers movie she once saw where a ridiculous number of people crammed into a tiny stateroom. He said he'd never seen that one and worked on spinning the piano-type stool higher.

"You think it wants to have its picture taken?" She was staring at the tiny, wriggling creature in the Baggie and puckered her lips, smiling.

Somehow she and Gregory managed to finally get in position and as she sat on his lap, he dropped in two coins. They waited for the red light to signal them and when it did, they made funny faces as the machine buzzed and exploded light in their faces.

The groaning booth recorded their four poses in under thirty seconds: one with no expression, the second with tongues out, the third with crossed eyes and crazy smiles, the last with them kissing and her holding the fish up proudly, as if it were a newborn child.

When it was done, they laughed and freed themselves from the booth, waiting outside for the photos.

But they never came.

They waited ten minutes. Twenty. And finally they walked away impatiently passing Madame Destiny and wishing her a good life. She seemed to move in the shifting colors of the arcade, head turning slightly inside the glass box, eyes flashing dread.

The two of them bought tickets for the house of mirrors and as they disappeared into its maze, a small boy eating a chili-dog walked by the photo booth. He heard a developing sound and watched as a narrow strip of photos slipped from the booth into a metal catch.

He took the photos and peered at them curiously, biting into his chili-dog. In the first exposure was an expressionless young couple, in the second the woman looked scared, the man hostile. In the third, she looked terrified and he had a look of darkening imbalance. In the last exposure, the man looked satisfied while the woman looked dead, throat slit, eyes glassy.

The boy searched for the couple to give them the photos, but only found a Baggie with a dead goldfish in it as he stood in the empty lot of the market, shivering under neon.

OBSOLETE

DORA FROWNED.

"Tom... if I'm wrong, tell me I'm wrong."

Tom bit into his breakfast and sighed. He looked up at his wife and saw the concern on her sleepy, morning face.

"You're not wrong. I know we should do something." Tom neatened his tie at the collar, spread his hands candidly. "It's just that the kids..."

Dora's eyes caught flame.

"The kids? Are you kidding? Yesterday it ran the shower for Robert and the water was steaming hot. If I hadn't gotten home when I did..." she swept at the table with her balled napkin, sending crumbs everywhere.

"Honey, the crumbs," Tom spoke calmly.

"Let *it* worry about the crumbs. Maybe it can at least duplicate the functions of a broom." Dora's young face went rigid; intractable. "Tom, I want it out. It's a danger to my family."

"Honey, the man said it just takes some time for these helpers to adjust."

"Getting the kinks out? *No.* I won't stand for it. We bought one of these *things* to help out. Not to turn our lives upside down. Do you know what it's done wrong just this week? And I'm not talking about breaking dishes."

Tom rose and began to take his dishes to the sink. Dora stopped him with a gentle hand.

"I'm sorry. I'll get the dishes. It's just I'm so nervous about that thing. I've never been close to one...please, let's get rid of it. It's not like us."

Tom took his wife into his arms and stroked her gently. "I'll take care of it before I leave for work."

Outside, it was kneeled over a cluster of flowers, trimming them. Tom walked up behind as he did every morning on his way to the garage.

"Stop gardening, please."

It did, lifting the nippers away from the stems, waiting.

"You'll have to leave." He faltered for a tense second. "My wife and I don't want you here any longer."

It remained motionless.

"It just isn't working out...we'll have to take you back to the center. Maybe they can find you another family."

The helper nodded and Tom's mouth tightened.

"I wish things had worked out."

He walked to the garage and pulled away in a cloud of exhaust. It washed over the helper which accidentally clamped the nippers onto its fingers causing red blood to run.

As it wept, one of the children ran up and stared at it through a single, dilating lens.

"What's wrong?" asked the little girl, synthesized voice concerned. "What's that stuff coming out of your finger?"

The old woman wadded cloth around the running blood and smiled a lonely hurt; a perfectly built replica of a human and one of the last five hundred remaining, waiting to be scrapped.

RED

HE KEPT WALKING.

The day was hot and miserable and he wiped his forehead. Up another twenty feet, he could make out more. Thank God. Maybe he'd find it all. He picked up the pace and his breathing got thick. He struggled on, remembering his vow to himself to go through with this, not stopping until he was done. Maybe it had been a mistake to ask this favor. But it was the only way he could think of to work it out. Still, maybe it had been a mistake.

He felt an edge in his stomach as he stopped and leaned down to what was at his feet. He grimaced, lifted it into the large canvas bag he carried, wiped his hands and moved on. The added weight in the bag promised of more and he felt somehow better. He had found most of what he was looking for in the first mile. Only a half more to go, to convince himself, to be sure.

To not go insane.

It was a nightmare for him to realize how far he'd gone this morning with no suspicion, no clue. He held the bag more tightly and walked on. Ahead, the forms who waited got bigger; closer. They stood with arms crossed, people gathered, complaining, behind them.

They would have to wait.

He saw something a few yards up, swallowed and walked

closer. It was everywhere and he shut his eyes, trying not to see how it must have been. But he saw it all. Heard it in his head. The sounds were horrible and he couldn't make them go away. Nothing would go away, until he had everything; he was certain of that. Then his mind would at least have some chance to find a place of comfort. To go on.

He bent down and picked up what he could, then walked on, scanning ahead. The sun was beating down and he felt his shirt soaking with sweat under the arms and on his back. He was nearing the forms who waited when he stopped, seeing something halfway between himself and them. It had lost its shape, but he knew what it was and couldn't step any closer. He placed the bag down and slowly sat cross-legged on the baking ground, staring. His body began to shake.

A somber looking man walked to him and carefully picked up the object, placing it in the canvas bag and cinching the top. He gently coaxed the weeping man to stand and the man nodded through tears. Together, they walked toward the others who were glancing at watches and losing patience.

"But I'm not finished," the man cried. His voice broke and his eyes grew hot and puffy. "Please...I'll go crazy...just a little longer?"

The somber looking man hated what was happening and made the decision. "I'm sorry, sir. Headquarters said I could only give you the half-hour you asked for. That's all I can do. It's a very busy road."

The man tried to struggle away but was held more tightly. He began to scream and plead and two middle-aged women who were waiting watched uncomfortably.

"Whoever allowed this should be reported," said one, shaking her head critically. "The poor man is ready to have a nervous breakdown. It's cruel."

The other said she'd heard they felt awful for the man, whose little girl had grabbed on when he'd left for work that morning. The girl had gotten caught and he'd never known.

They watched the officer approaching with the crying man

who he helped into the hot squad car. Then, the officer grabbed the canvas bag and as it began to drip red onto the blacktop, he gently placed it into the trunk beside the mangled tricycle.

The backed-up cars began to honk and traffic was waved on as the man was driven away.

BEHOLDER

CARRIE STARED at the faded art gallery as if seeing something strange in a mirror for the first time.

The front window was soaped and a high banner draped where Greene's sign had hung only one week back. In perfectly painted letters, it read: UNDER NEW MANAGEMENT.

She shook her head. The gallery had been doing well enough last time she'd been in. Why hadn't Greene said something about leaving?

Switching off the car radio, she got out, walked to the gallery's door and tried the locked knob. Glancing for the buzzer, she located a button and pressed.

Footsteps approached within and the door was noisily unsecured. Carrie tried again and as the hinges squeaked, she entered, grasping her purse.

As she walked in, the door slammed and she spun toward it. She was startled by a voice from the gallery's rear.

"Sorry," said the voice, "it's only the wind."

She slowly approached the counter. To either side of the musty gallery were frames, paintings, etchings and prints. The same stuff which hadn't sold since she'd moved in three months back. Odd that Greene hadn't taken anything with him, she thought.

"It's why I keep the door locked. The breezes knock it open and shut all day."

He stood behind the counter in a vanilla-colored silk shirt, hair long and black. His face was classically handsome and easily more than fifty.

"Are you the new owner?" she asked, nerves still shaken.

He extended a friendly hand and Carrie noticed the heavy rings. Too thick to be a woman's, too delicate to be a man's.

"As a matter-of-fact, I only took it over recently." He looked at her carefully. "My name is Christian."

Carrie met his hand and was reassured by its warmth. He shared a look with her and they both smiled.

"Carrie," she offered. "What happened to Mr. Greene?"

"Decided to travel through Europe. We made the exchange of the shop through the mail." He watched her. "He left rather quickly, I take it."

"Yes," said Carrie. "Didn't say a word."

They regarded each other in covert fascination.

"Are you an artist?" he finally asked, searching her face.

She smiled.

"No. But I've been wanting to do a painting. It struck me last night to do something about it. Isn't that odd?"

He acknowledged this with a small smile.

"Do you need supplies?"

"Everything," laughed Carrie. "I just moved here recently and left most of my things behind."

She looked off.

Getting a place in a small town was the best thing she'd done since everything had fallen apart. Broken marriages and a new place to start; her mother had been right.

He observed her, intently. "Well, I'm sure I'll have everything you'll need."

She brightened as he withdrew a large canvas from beneath the counter.

"About the right size?"

"Perfect."

Christian smiled and placed the canvas into a bag with other supplies he added to it. As he did, Carrie didn't notice him looking at her. Watching.

She peeked into the bag, took inventory and nodded in delight.

"Well," she began, taking inventory, "all that leaves is..."

"...paint," he finished for her, causing them to both laugh. "If I might suggest something," he said, "I was never able to find colors I wanted, when I painted, so I began to create my own. I have them here in the shop."

She looked into his eyes and felt her stomach tighten.

"How wonderful," she heard herself say, "I'd love to see them."

At that, Christian disappeared into the back of the gallery and reappeared with a jeweled box. Large enough to fit into her cupped hands, it was dull gold, with gems on sides and top.

"Please," he said, indicating the box, "I want you to see."

Carrie looked at him and hinged up the top without a word. Inside, a dozen, tear-shaped vials shone lustrous colors, the paints inside like heavenly syrups.

Carrie held each vial to the light of the soaped window, causing each to brand regal prisms upon her face.

"They're like pieces of a rainbow," she whispered.

"These paints are *very* special," he said. "You couldn't find others like them, anywhere in the world."

Carrie gently returned the vials to the box, carefully arranging them as they'd been. She looked at Christian and shook her head slightly.

"They're beautiful."

"Then you must have them."

"I...couldn't," she said, suddenly afraid. Something about the paints disturbed her. The tightening in her stomach returned.

Christian saw her confusion and took her hand.

"By knowing you'll create something with my paints, I gain something." He held her hand, imploringly. "It's a kind of circular intimacy; a continuation."

Carrie looked at him, feeling haunted and drawn into something she could neither understand nor resist. She could only watch without protest as Christian placed the paints in her bag, smiling.

Waiting for her to begin.

It was past midnight when Carrie set up the easel and canvas. A white moon had lifted itself over a bank of clouds and its light brought shapes to the fields outside her bedroom window.

She sipped tea and sat on a stool, in her nightgown, before the canvas. The house was silent and cooperatively tranquil; wishing to aid in her creation.

She had set the vials Christian gave her on a small tray next to the canvas and poised the brush in her hand, eyes searching outside for an idea; an inspiration.

The meadows and trees, outside the window, and beyond, into open country, were in slumber, darkness hiding their trunks and leaves.

Carrie took a sip of tea.

What to paint, she wondered, staring at the taut canvas? She sipped again until the view outside drew her eye. The window was covered by French doors, the swaying fields beyond a restive bay of green. The room, itself, with windows prominent and fields as background, could make something nice, she thought. Worth a try.

She dipped the brush into a vial of jewel-brown paint, and began.

With its shimmering milkiness, she outlined the room, the French doors, the balcony outside and several of the trees which napped in distant meadows.

She rinsed the brush and with the vial of twinkling, sapphire blue, finished the sky outside and colored the crystal panes of the French doors.

She shivered and took another drink of tea. It was getting cold outside and she took a sweater from her closet. Pulling it on, she began to study the painting. It needed something in the foreground.

She closed her eyes, trying to visualize what would look right.

They opened, quickly.

Of course!

Immediately, the brush was dipped into the pearl black paint and Carrie began to outline a bed. First the headboard and baseboard, finally the coverlet, yet to be colored in.

As she watched her hand moving, she looked beyond it to the forming painting.

It was starting to come alive and she could feel its rhythms.

Its pulse.

As she painted the branches of the trees, shifting and straining in the imaginary winds of the painting, she heard the wind outside begin to stir. It rose as she painted in the detail of each branch. Leaves rustled against the French windows, in tangled flight.

She painted a moon leaning casually in the black sky of the painting, and the blowing leaves outside her own window began to faintly glimmer. But she paid little attention to these curiosities, her hands and eyes not drifting much from the painting.

As if knowing each movement, she rinsed her brush, immersed it into the proper vial and painted in something further, rushing the work to its completion.

She repeated this over and over, painting the room in richer detail: an antique dresser, an arched doorway, a blazing fireplace.

With the completion of the painted fireplace, her own bedroom filled with the sound of crackling logs, the odor of burning pine.

She continued to paint, unaware; possessed by urges which had long since taken over. Disconnected from the room, she was linked only to the painting, now.

Her hands moved rapidly over the canvas, as if conducting some mad symphony, and she began to paint someone in the bed, under the silk comforter. The vials were quickly emptying as Carrie painted faster, giving the form in the bed more detail. There were long, tapered arms. Hair like her own.

Her favorite gown…

Her breathing stumbled as she looked at the face. *It was her.* There was no question.

Without reacting, she began to paint with renewed focus. More detail, ever more detail. She added a blue taper. Then another. Both in beautiful sconces on the painting's bedside tables, flames slithering.

As she did this, the electric lights in her own room went suddenly off. Yet, some strange glow remained, mysteriously filling the room.

Several of the bewitching paints were now emptied from their vials and few remained. In the vial of translucent blood-red, a single drop rested at the bottom.

The painting was nearly done and the room Carrie had rendered was stunning. It was lit by tapers and firelight and its opened French windows bid entry to midnight breezes.

She could feel her own hair blowing and as she looked over at the window in her room, she shuddered.

It was still closed.

She felt herself react in fear but kept painting. As she did, noticing almost nothing of what she drew, she trembled, feeling a warm hand touch her face.

She looked at the painting and nearly screamed.

She had painted a man's hand gently resting, in the painting, on her face.

In captivation, her brush began anew, more slowly, as if caressing the remaining portions of canvas.

Without her conscious guidance, the brush painted in the man's legs, and she felt warm legs pressing against her own.

As she painted shoulders and strong forearms, she breathed a male scent and could feel the beginnings of an embrace.

And though she fought the painting's seductions, afraid of what was coming, her brush continued emptying vial after vial.

She could now feel warm breath on her neck and a naked body laying next to her own, stroking it, just as in the painting. Her eyes closed completely and she could no longer see what she was painting. Nor could she separate what she painted from what she felt herself. The two places and moments were merging.

Joining.

She felt sensual breathing beginning to lower toward her mouth and heard her name being whispered as her brush dipped into the last available paint.

The single drop of red.

In slow motion, her arm arced from the tray of paints to the canvas and sought a specific spot.

As she painted in the man's lips with the single drop of red, she felt full lips lowering onto hers, warmly covering her mouth. Looking up into the man's face, the room in which she painted went suddenly still.

On the floor, the brush had fallen. There were also empty paint vials, which had scattered uselessly. Little else. Except for the empty gown which lay beneath the easel.

Left behind.

"They're beautiful, aren't they?" said a friendly voice, which approached the young woman.

"They're very strange," she said, studying the paintings. "You can't make out the man's face in any of them."

He looked at her, watching every detail while the museum tour whispered by the small exhibit area. "Perhaps he preferred it that way."

She nodded and began to walk away.

"Excuse me," he said, "do you paint?"

She looked at him and stopped, a bit intrigued.

And as the dozens of paintings watched, with trapped eyes pleading for him to stop, Christian withdrew the golden box from his coat pocket.

DEAD END

IT WAS A PERFECT DAY for a drive. There was a blue sky with full white clouds that floated carelessly, drifting in slow motion with the wind. The brisk air was cool and clean from the rain the night before.

I floored the Porsche, and Annie and I were thrown to the left by the small curve. The tires slid slightly on the moist pavement.

"Careful," said Annie.

"Right," I answered. She was looking at the map. "What's our next move?" I asked, curving more tenderly into another turn in the canyon road.

"I think we go right on the next street."

I looked at the street sign coming up. "Evans?"

"That's it," she said. We turned onto the street and followed its curves further up into the canyon.

We were just above L.A. and the view, looking out over the city, was gorgeous. The lines of the buildings were sharply focused and the tinted windows returned our stares with gleaming clarity. With its smog washed briefly away, Los Angeles was striking.

"It's a nice place when it doesn't have a blanket of muck all over it," I said. Annie didn't respond, and reached to turn on the radio. She played with the dial until a station surfaced. "Up ahead we should be taking a left," she said.

"What's the street?" I shifted into third as the road steepened.

"Parkmore," she said, turning up the volume.

"Parkmore," I repeated, as the Porsche sped around more curves.

On either side of us were what the L.A. realtors like to call "Hillside Hideaways." They were stylishly expensive houses and apartments which were built onto the side of the mountains. They all overlooked expansive and inspirational views of the city and, from where we were, the ocean. It was a thin blue strip at the ground's end, in the distance.

"These roads remind me of Europe," I said, sliding my hands around the steering wheel, "especially with the architecture up here. Every house looks like a decorator designed it." Annie pointed up ahead, momentarily lowering her map. "Parkmore," she said. I nodded, and when I got to Parkmore, "Left?" I said.

"Yes," she answered.

We were heading up again. Farther and farther above the city. Annie and I didn't talk much, though. It had been that way for almost four months. Maybe more. Ever since she got back from the hospital. That day.

That awful day.

The doctor said we could try again, but Annie seemed without hope. She kept saying she felt cheated. She wanted to start again but was afraid. And the apartment seemed to be making it worse. When she finally found a new place in the paper, I was for the idea. She needed something.

We both did.

"What did they tell you?" I asked, making conversation.

"Not much. Two-bedroom. View. Fireplace."

"They sound friendly?"

"I guess. Damn, I'm losing the station." She began turning the knob again, and amid static, found a weak classical station. It sounded like a piece I recognized. "Respighi," I suggested.

"Maybe," she said, cranking down her window. "It's hard to say."

"Yeah," I agreed, "it is."

"I hate classical music," she said, staring out the window.

I raced the Porsche's engine and we came to a rise up ahead. I couldn't see what was on the other side. I slowed down and we rose over the rise, down the other side. Ahead was a circular dead end. Nothing had been built there. It was deserted and still. "Terrific," I said, stopping the Porsche.

"You blaming me?" she said immediately.

"No," I said with a smile, "these roads are just confusing. It's easy to get fouled up. One looks like another."

"But I was giving directions, right? So whose fault would it be?"

"Hey, come on, that's not what I meant, babe."

Her mouth stiffened. Her eyes looked away from mine. "It seems recently like it's always my fault," she said.

"I don't feel that way. Let's take a look at that map."

I slowly took the map from her hands and retraced our steps. It looked like we had done everything right. It was just that the street we were looking for was missing. It was supposed to be where the dead end was. "Clearsite," I said.

"What?"

"That's the street the house is on. Clearsite Terrace."

"Well, where is it?" she demanded.

"Good question." I was trying to see if maybe we hadn't taken the wrong street at the bottom of the hill. It was possible. If so, we had gotten started wrongly and somehow managed to hit a couple of the correct streets.

"God, haven't we had enough problems this week. And now this," said Annie, opening her purse and taking out a cigarette.

"Don't worry. We'll find it. Let's keep looking. It's gotta be around here somewhere," I said, pushing the lighter on the dash in for her.

As I sped back over the road which had led to the dead end, I looked quickly over at Annie, smoking. Her expression wasn't there. It was as if Annie, the Annie I had fallen in love with and married so long ago, had emptied out. Maybe when she lost the baby it started. All her love was in that baby and all her love went with it, it seemed. She never even knew the baby. Never even saw it. But somehow she changed. Really changed.

"You don't like it when I smoke. Why don't you just say so...?"

"Annie, if you want to smoke..."

"I know you can't stand it. I know you think it isn't good for my health. Of course, it never was. Maybe that's why..."

I interrupted, quickly. "Annie, that's not what I'm thinking. Please drop it. What's that street up ahead?"

She took a drag on her cigarette and checked the map against the street name. "Ginger Lane," she said. "It's supposed to be Rossmoor, according to the map. We're getting lost."

"No, we're not," I said. "Here, let me see the map."

I pulled over and she handed it to me. Looking out at the city, I could see that the late afternoon was fading to nightfall. I ran my finger over the street names repeatedly, but things weren't connecting. The streets we had driven up didn't seem to be where I remembered them. I was beginning to think maybe we *were* lost. "Look, this is ridiculous," I said, "let's just go down and start over."

Annie was smoking another cigarette. She took the map, opened the glove compartment, crammed it in. "What do you mean, just go down?"

"Simple. We'll follow one of these roads back to the main canyon road. Once we're down, we'll come up and find the place more carefully."

She said nothing, but nodded hesitant agreement. The idea seemed to at least meet her approval, though it obviously didn't please her. Her mood was changing. It had darkened. I think admitting we were lost made her feel defenseless.

I quickly steered the Porsche down a street we'd initially travelled up. As we swerved downward through the hushed road, branches from the overhanging trees brushed against the targa roof.

Two or three cars passed us going the other way, but it was hard to see the passengers inside. There was no detail to the faces.

Just indistinct, staring shipments of people peering out at us. Then back at the road.

I spotted something familiar ahead.

"Evans."

"That's where we started," said Annie.

Now we're getting somewhere, I thought.

At Evans, I made a left, reversing my original right turn. As we drove down Evans, I saw something I hadn't recalled—a rise.

It sat, stolid and immense; a mute imposition of lifeless road, risen from asphalt. Mist nestled at its top.

I stopped. Annie and I looked at it, then at each other.

"That wasn't there," she said.

"No," I said, becoming upset and frowning.

"Well, please forgive my stupid directions, darling."

I rubbed my temples with my palms. "Annie, please," I whispered.

"I forgot," she said, with a sharp edge in her voice, "there's only supposed to be one sensitive person in this relationship, right?" She blew a self-certain stream of smoke out the window and the wind caught it.

I ignored her. "Let's see what's on the other side."

I floored the Porsche and it quickly lifted us through the mist, up and over the rise. I slowed down and brought the car to an immediate stop.

I swallowed as I looked around. We had come to another dead end. Only it looked exactly like the first one. The same formations of tumbleweeds and towering silver streetlamps. Even the four lots, empty, ready to be built on, were the same. The city, in the distance, was beginning to flicker awake with fuzzy lights. We were high up, again. Yet we'd been driving downhill for several minutes. It made no sense. "Does this look like the other dead end to you?" I asked carefully.

Annie moved uncomfortably in her seat. "Asking my advice?"

I sighed. I didn't want to argue. "All right. Yes."

"I think whoever gave me these instructions must be playing a practical joke or something. I don't see how we could go wrong with just a few streets."

"Me neither... but we did."

"You mean *I* did..."

I grabbed Annie's shoulder. "Look, we're both confused and tired. There's no need to turn everything I say into an issue. Until we get home, why don't you lay off, huh?"

"Like I said," Annie was pulling away from my hand, "only one of us is supposed to have feelings."

"All right, you want to make things harder, go ahead. Just don't talk to me," I said, screeching the tires as I turned from the dead end and headed back over the rise.

On the other side, the mist seemed thicker around us. It made the feeling of gnawing disorientation worse. I squinted pensively.

There had to be a small street I had missed that would lead back to the main canyon. I had probably just missed it.

As I drove, I glanced at her from the corner of my eye. Her arms were crossed and she'd pulled the collar of her jacket high. It was impossible to see anything but her eyes. And even though wide open, they seemed closed to everything. How could it have happened so quickly? So totally?

I couldn't remember the last time we'd laughed together. Or said we loved each other. The things that were once all we needed and everything we had. Somewhere, they had just gotten lost. I don't even know why. But it made me sad.

Terribly sad.

God, we needed that new house. To begin again; try and forget.

"Slow down," she demanded. "There's a couple walking up ahead." As the Porsche drew closer to them, I braked and Annie rolled down her window.

"Excuse me," she said.

The couple turned to face us. They looked to be in their eighties. Their faces were deeply lined, their eyes murky and curious. The mist gathered at them as they spoke.

"What's the problem?" asked the old man, firmly planting his walking stick and peering into the Porsche.

"I'm afraid we're lost," I said. "We're trying to get back to the main canyon."

The old man laughed and looked at the old woman. She smiled.

"Lost, eh?"

"Right," I said, leaning toward Annie's seat so I could see him.

"Well, I'll tell you, folks, your best bet is to take that first right down there and follow it a mile or so until you come to a stop sign. When you get to that sign, that's the canyon."

The old woman breathed heavily and kneeled down a bit. Her hair was thin, teeth brown. She grinned at us. "You folks visiting someone up here?"

"We're looking for a house we were interested in renting," said Annie. "It's on Clearsite Terrace."

The couple looked at her and their mouths twitched a bit at the sides. Their smiles fell and they nodded. The old man tapped his walking stick once or twice on the pavement. He licked liver-spotted lips and grabbed weakly at the Porsche's door as he looked in one final time.

"Well, like I said, take that first right. It'll take you right to where you're heading."

"Right to it," repeated his wife.

I looked at them appreciatively. "Thanks," I said, with a relieved smile. "We'll be happy to get down from here, I'll tell you."

He squinted at me knowingly and the old woman took his arm. They straightened and walked away from the car, talking quietly between themselves, then disappeared down a sleepy lane, swallowed in mist.

Annie rolled up her window and I pulled the Porsche away from the shoulder, racing toward the street the old man indicated. The interior of the car was cold and Annie shivered slightly as I took the turn.

"The heater," she said.

I slid the heat controls on, and from beneath our legs came a comforting blast of hot air. It blew my pant legs slightly, and I tightened my grip on the wheel as we moved quickly through the street. I reached to turn on the lights and noticed the gas gauge was almost on empty. Outside, the sunset was near end.

"It's going to be dark in a few minutes," she said accusingly. "We're just wasting our time up here. The owners of that house have probably already rented it."

I was looking at the needle of the gas gauge. It was almost completely leaning against the E, bouncing only in response to the road. I was certain the couple had given us correct directions. I flipped on the headlights and clicked the high beam up, brought my face to the windshield, peering ahead. The road was new.

Different.

This had to be right.

The old man had probably lived up there for years. He and his wife seeing hundreds of lost people. Helping them.

The road suddenly dipped down and I shifted to second and let the clutch out to slow us. Annie stiffly grabbed the dashboard for support. "You're driving like a maniac," she said. "Didn't you hear what I said before? We're wasting our time up here."

I didn't take my eyes off the road. It was curving, wrapping itself around the circumference of the mountain. The mist all around us had curdled to fog.

"I know," I said. "I'm trying to get down."

"Well, you're doing one hell of a lousy job," she said, voice raised, cigarette about to be lit.

I pressed my lips together. No point talking.

Annie watched me as I drove. She ran a hand through her hair as I froze my eyes on the road.

Jarringly, from out of the fog, a tiny figure jumped in front of the headlights and I slammed on the brakes. It was a small dog. Its eyes stared into the headlights and shone back at us. We had come within inches of it. I honked the horn and it stood motionless for a second before scurrying away.

"God, you almost killed it!" she yelled.

"I didn't see it," I said, not looking at her.

"You're driving like you're crazy," she said. "What do you expect?"

"I thought you were in a hurry."

"Is your idea of hurrying getting us both killed? What the hell is the matter with you?"

I held down the horn for several seconds, cutting her off. I released it and looked at her; seethed my words. "What is goddamn wrong with me is you. I am doing the best I can to get us down from this labyrinth and you're not helping. Either shut up or get out of the car and walk."

Annie said nothing. There was a brooding finality to her silence as she looked away.

I put the Porsche in first and driving the RPMs to redline, popped the clutch. The tires screamed hotly against the pavement and I looked at the speedometer as we sped faster and faster around curves. We were going over eighty.

But the farther we traveled the more we got nowhere. The main canyon was nowhere in sight. Just more stretches of quiet, foggy streets and no people.

Impatiently, I slammed the gas pedal to the floor. The engine exhaled a guttural moan and the car lurched forward. We made an acute left turn, and looming up ahead of the car, at the end of the straightaway we were on, was a rise. I clenched my teeth when I saw it, but didn't stop.

I shoved the gear box into second, and the Porsche howled in the evening air as we ascended the rise and plummeted down its other side.

My stomach fluttered at what I saw.

The silver streetlights weren't lit and the tumbleweeds hadn't moved. The lots sat still, the chilly breeze of nightfall sweeping at them.

"What the *hell* is going on!" Annie screamed.

"I don't know," I said.

"This is the same goddamned dead end!"

I looked out at the city and watched as it began to glow in the blackening sky. The Porsche idled reassuringly and Annie impulsively opened her door and got out. "Idiot!" she said, with a stabbing fury. "Is there *anything* left you can do right?"

She threw the door shut and I watched as she crossed the wet beams of the headlights. She walked up the slope on one side of the lot closest to the car. It was becoming dark, and she was only a silhouette by the time she got to the top of the lot, looking toward the city.

For a way down, I suppose.

I didn't try to get out and stop her.

It would have been no use.

She didn't listen to me anymore. There was so little left between us. Nothing, really.

We didn't even know each other.

I looked up at one of the streetlight posts and my eyes fixed on the sign which hung upon it. I hadn't smoked in months, but I took one of Annie's cigarettes from the pack she'd left on the dash. I lit it, and as I took the first drag, the night went suddenly quiet. The engine had stopped. Out of gas.

I turned off the lights and sat in the leather seat, waiting for the car to get cold. It would take only minutes in the night.

It was so cold outside.

I shook a little and tried to warm my hands. It didn't do much good. I looked out the window and couldn't see Annie anymore, up on the lot. She must have gone farther. Trying to see down.

The cigarette burned hot in my mouth as the moon began to light the sign. In simple black letters, against the yellow, square background, it moved a little in the stirring wind.

It said DEAD END, and I couldn't take my eyes off it.

The cigarette went out and I threw it on the floor.

My eyes began to water and burn.

But it wasn't tears. It was just the mountain and the dark and being lost and cold.

It just felt like there was no way out for a minute or so.

And then another minute joined it.

And then another.

COMMUTERS

MORNING TRAFFIC snailed along the freeway, taillights pulsing splinters on rainy lanes.

Steve sighed, trying to ignore the tidal wave that splashed across his LTD as a Greyhound cut him off. He turned the wipers high and watched them rock ... *slosh, wipe, slosh, wipe*; a hypnotist's pendulum. It was a wonder he didn't just drift off sometimes and ...

He sat straighter, pressed in his newest morning cassette, turned up the volume and glanced at the plastic box. The title stared at him:

TAKING RISKS, TAKING CONTROL

He turned the volume higher, finding the voice on the tape relaxing. He enjoyed using his commute constructively ever since Karen suggested it their first year of marriage.

"Make something of our lives," she'd encouraged sweetly once the honeymoon was over and married life lulled him into its polite trance.

She never missed the chance to remind him good husbands struggled and fought to improve themselves. And they achieved for those they loved.

A bigger house, more money. A better life.

Last message of the night, first message of the day; the gentle litany was always there.

He turned on the de-fogger and listened closely to a recommendation the tape made about being open to new ideas as a red Honda Prelude pulled along side, throwing water against his passenger door. He looked over irritably and saw a feminine hand rub a circle on the fogged glass of the driver's door. A woman's eyes checked the rearview, then glanced at him.

He tried to see what she looked like but somebody was honking and Steve realized he'd accidentally swerved toward another lane while watching her eyes. He jerked the wheel straight and glanced over once again but her window had already re-fogged and she was gone. He sighed as her Prelude pulled ahead several car lengths.

The cassette was talking about embracing risk-taking opportunities and Steve thought about the client meeting he'd be running in half an hour; the deal he'd stalked for over a year. If it went well, he and Karen would get everything and he wanted all to go perfectly. Make the right impression. Succeed.

Be a good husband.

He could almost hear Karen's loving voice, gently shoving him closer to the edge and tried to ignore the image. His lane was moving faster and he glanced to his right where the Prelude lady was now beside him, peeking through a porthole she made with a circling palm on her driver's window. He could see more of her than before and noticed her hair style was plain, her face done with little make-up. He watched her from the corner of his eye and decided she seemed intent on appearing unobvious. On fitting in.

Then it struck him as if a whisper from across a room.

Maybe she was like everyone else who rode the tiresome rapids of this freeway, dutifully dressed and on time, glaring anxiously at wristwatches and fearing everything would be lost if they didn't clock-in at nine. Though Steve fought the sensation every morning, he couldn't help sometimes feeling surrounded by well-dressed, well-disguised terror which moved in lines of dread, responsibilities and obligations making their fingers drum, their ulcers bleed.

Rain fell harder and the cassette was telling him triumph and risks went hand in hand: there was no such thing in life as safety. Only carefully rehearsed and memorized behaviors. Patterns. Habits.

Tapes. Just like the one he was listening to.

Only he decided this one didn't feel comfortable to him, its ideas uneasily liberating. He sensed risks weren't the way to get ahead for people like him. Hard work was. He and Karen had even talked about it at length. He enjoyed following rules.

Even though he hated the commute. And getting up early.

But then everybody did.

Sure his blood pressure was a little on the high side and he smoked too much. And he didn't always sleep as well as he should, and sometimes late at night he'd slip out of bed, go into the bathroom, turn the water on and just listen to it so he wouldn't hear the fears that turned on in his head like rows of stoveburners.

But then everybody had moments, didn't they?

He glanced over at the lady in the Prelude and noticed she seemed to be crying, holding Kleenex to her cheeks. Her expression trembled as she gripped the wheel.

The tape was suggesting that taking chances was the only way to have something to show for your life when the final moments slipped away and all the inventory had been stacked, shelved and accounted for.

Steve wasn't sure why, but he felt suddenly concerned for the woman. Without thinking, he honked at her. He honked again and she glanced over, features guarded by wrinkled Kleenex. He didn't know what to do and felt ridiculous: an unwelcome invader in an LTD.

He realized he had to do something and with an embarrassed expression hit his electric-window button. As the wet glass lowered, she was there looking at him, her own window sliding down at the same speed.

They stared at each other and he instantly knew he liked her face; it was kind and soft and her reddened eyes seemed somehow happy to see him. She wasn't really pretty but there was a vulnerable quality he'd never seen in Karen's eyes. The sound of splashing traffic forced him to yell,

"Are you okay?"

She shook her head yes, then looked away and back at him, this time shaking no, eyes frightened and sad. Her expression struck something inside him and he cupped a hand to his mouth and yelled words to her that stunned him.

He was asking her to follow him.

She didn't acknowledge it for a moment, glancing away, absorbed in her tears and the insane, kayak paddling of morning traffic. But she finally looked over at him and nodded, and together they fought the steaming freeway for another quarter mile, taking the next offramp.

They parked under a huge freeway bridge and he got out of his LTD and ran through puddles to her car, shoes soaking, schedule in irreversible jeopardy. She had her window re-closed and when he peered in she looked out cautiously at then slowly slid it down; a defensive barricade being lowered. Her engine was idling and the exhaust pillowed them in oily white.

He stood there, not knowing what to say and they both stared at each other, seeming to sense the condition of the other's life. The trapped, contracted-for agreement of jobs and marriage and relationships with people that didn't care about them; what they were deep inside, where no one could see. The arrangements of time and convenience that a life, any life, could become. The empty experiences and decisions that most often served efficiency, rarely a heart.

He saw those things in her face.

And he was sure she saw them in his.

And under that bridge, with hundreds of tons of cars and lives and people and schedules and emptiness roaring overhead, they smiled at each other and he got in her car and they drove away together.

GRADUATION

January 15
Dear Mom and Dad:

IT HAS BEEN an expectedly hectic first week; unpacking, organizing, getting scheduled in classes, and of course, fraternizing with the locals to secure promise of later aid should I need it. I don't think I will. My room is nice though it has a view which Robert Frost would scoff at; perhaps a transfer to a better location later this semester is possible. We'll see.

I had a little run-in with the administration when I arrived; a trivial technicality. Something about too much luggage. At least more than the other dormitory students brought with them. I cleared it up with a little glib know-how. As always. Some of the guys on my floor look as if they might be enjoyable and if I'm lucky maybe one or two will be interesting to talk to as well. But I can't chase after "impossible rainbows." That should sound familiar, Dad, it's from your private collection and has been gone over a "few" times. A few. But maybe this time, it's true. Anyway, the dormitory looks as if it's going to work out well. Pass the word to you-know-who. I'm sure it will interest him.

The dinner tonight was an absolute abomination. It could easily have been some medieval melange concocted by the college gardener utilizing lawn improver, machinist's oil, and ground-up old men. And I question even the quality of those ingredients. I may die tonight of poisoning. Maybe if I'm lucky it will strike quickly and leave no marks. Don't want Dad's old school to lose its accreditation after all. However, I'm a little concerned that the townspeople will be kept awake tonight by the sound of 247 "well-fed" freshmen looking at their reflections in the toilet bowl. Today while I was buying books an upper-classman called me green for not getting used ones. If he was in any way referring to the way my face looks right now, he should be hired by some psychic foundation. He can tell the future.

Anyway, Mom, I certainly do miss your cooking. Almost as much as I miss my stomach's equilibrium. Ugh.

The room gets cold early with the snow and all. But I have plenty of blankets (remember the excessive luggage? ... guessed it) so that poses no difficulty. I'll probably pick up a small heater next week, first free day I get. For now I'll manage with hot tea, the collected works of Charles Dickens, and warm memories of all of you back home. Until I write again, I send my love and an abundance of sneezes.

Here's looking achoo ...

Yours regurgitatively,

February 2
Dear Mom and Dad:

Greetings from Antarctica. It is unbelievably cold up here. If you can imagine your son as a hybrid between a Popsicle and a slab of marble, you've got the right idea, just make it a little colder. In a word, freezing. In another word, numbing. In two other words, liquid oxygen. I may be picking up that heater sooner than I thought. I see no future in becoming a glacier.

I met my professors today, all of whom seem interested and dedicated. My Calculus class might be a trifle dreary, but, then, numbers put a damper on things any way you look at it. The other courses look promising so far. Tell you-know-who that he-knows-who is genuinely excited about something. I'm sure he'll be cheered by that forecast of future involvements.

Burping is very popular in my wing of the dormitory and some of the guys have been explaining its physical principles to me, complete with sonic demonstrations to validate their theories. One guy, Jim, who looks a little like a bull dog with slightly bigger eyes (and a much bigger stomach) apparently holds the record in two prestigious areas: he drinks the most and belches the loudest. For your own personal information files, he also seems to know the fewest words a person can possess and still communicate with. I estimate that the exact number of words is a high one-digit counting number, but I could still be going too easily on him. His belches, however, are enormously awesome. He is able (he whispered to me when I bumped into his drunken body in the hallway last night) to make time stand still temporarily with one of his burps.

Furthermore (he said), that would be one of his lesser efforts. Were he to launch a truly prize-winning belch (he said) civilization as we know it would be obliterated and the earth's atmosphere rendered noxious for 2,000 years. Personally, I feel he exaggerates a bit. Maybe 1,500 years.

Jim doesn't stop burping until 1 or 2 in the morning, which makes studying a degree harder. It's like having a baby in the dorm, with Jim erupting and gurgling into the a.m. hours. Except that he weighs 300 pounds. But I'm learning to live with it. Occasionally, he gets to be more than a petty annoyance and I get upset, but it's really nothing to worry about. So tell you-know-who to not put himself into a state. I'm fine.

If we could harness the secret of Jim's aberration and regulate it at timed intervals perhaps Yellowstone Park would be interested. Oh well, he'll probably quiet down soon. I miss you all a lot and send my fondest love. Until I thaw out again, bye for now.

Bundlingly yours …

P.S. Avoid telling you-know-who I'm "cold" up here. He has this thing about that word.

February 22
Dear Mom and Dad:

An enlivening new roommate has entered my monastic quarters. He is slight in frame and says very little; a simple kind of person with a dearth of affinities, except for cheese, which he loves. I call him Hannibal owing to his fearlessly exploratory nature. You see Hannibal, while not easy to detect, is very much present. He comes out to mingle only during the evening. The late evening. More precisely, that part of the evening when I like to try and catch some sleep. Hannibal is evidently on a different schedule than I.

In short, I have mouse trouble.

Hannibal, in all fairness, is but one of the offenders. He is joined each evening by a host of other raucous marauders who squeal and scratch until dawn, determined to disturb my rest. They're actually quite cute, but are, regardless of angelic appearances, a steadily unappreciated annoyance.

I mentioned my visitors to some of the other students in the dormitory and they said I wasn't the only victim of the whiskered nocturnal regime. They advised setting traps and, failing that, to use a poison which can be purchased from the student store. It is rumored to yield foolproof results. I know it sounds altogether like a cross borrowing from Walt Disney and an Edgar Allan Poe story, but, regrettably, I must do something.

As an alternate plan, I thought of possibly speaking with a brainy flutist I know from orchestra class, who is quite talented. Whether or not he would care to revivify a Gothic tale simply for the benefit of my slumbrous tranquility is something we will have to discuss. Also the question of playing and walking at the same time may come up. But I'll try to circumvent that aspect. It's a slightly off-beat gig but it seems an improvement on the other method. I'll speak with him.

My classes are going fairly well, with no serious laggings in any subject despite the effects of Jim and Hannibal's henchmen upon my alertness. Thanks for the letter and a very special thanks for those fantastic cookies, Mom. They were delicious. You really made my day. And the travelling scent of your generosity made me quite sought after for a "little sample" of what food can really taste like. Jim went ape over them and said he wouldn't mind taking the whole next box off my hands. Which is something like a man with no legs admitting that he, occasionally, limps. Good old Jim. He'll probably eat himself to death one day. Although it would take him at least two days to do it right.

In light of the popularity of your largess, I have determined that everybody else must have the same immense regard for the school cook I do. He is acquiring a definite reputation, the likes of which has been shared by a handful of historical figures. Lizzie Borden, Jack the Ripper. The man has no regard for the human taste bud. All in all, I'm convinced that our chef will most assuredly go to hell.

Anyway, Mom, thanks again for the cookies. They were eaten with rapturous abandon. And you may have saved several students from ulcers. What better compliment? All my love to everyone back home. Including you-know-who.

Thwarted by burps, squeaks,
and bad food …

P.S. I think Jim (our resident sulphur spring) finally knows what it's like being kept up at night. He too has mouse trouble. (At least someone will visit him.)

March 9

Dear Mom and Dad:

Got in a small amount of trouble today as a result of being late to class and complicating matters by arguing with my professor over a dumb thing he said about me.

You see, in Philosophy I, as it is taught by Marshall B. Francis, you are not allowed an impregnable viewpoint. It must always be open to comment. And he says he likes to analyze. I told him he likes to shred and butcher. Whereupon he requested a "formal presentation of my personal philosophy of life's purpose."

Since, as you know, my philosophy responds unfavorably to direct assault, I refused. Mistake number one.

He told me if I didn't cooperate he'd have me leave the class and withdraw all credit from my participation thus far. I thought this unfair, so we started yelling at one another and in the clouded ferocity of our exchanges I accidentally slashed him on the cheek with my pen. It wasn't deep, but it scared him a lot. It wasn't at all like it may seem; I say that only because I know what you're probably thinking. Believe me, it was just a freak accident with one lost temper responding to another.

We talked in the infirmary later and he said he understood and would allow me a second chance. After that kindness, I volunteered my philosophy without hesitation (rather sheepishly), and he smiled at my completion of the apologies. He said that sometimes you have to be willing to fight for your beliefs and that he respected my actions in class, saving the accident, of course. I think we'll be great friends by the end of the year (if he doesn't get infected and die); however, philosophers consider life to be a danger so I guess it wouldn't surprise him too much.

It is still very cold with no trace of warmth. Jim continues to noisily burn (or is it burp) the midnight oil much to the chagrin of everyone in the dorm. If a sonic boom occurred during the evening, it would be completely overlooked. Buried.

Once again, my love to all of you back home, and I sure would like to hear from you, so please write. Better not tell you-know-who what happened to me today. He'll get the wrong impression. He has enough people to worry about as it is.

With new-found philosophy,

P.S. Hannibal is no longer with me. He and his men are squeaking across those great Alps in the sky. That poison really was foolproof.

March 18
Dear Mom and Dad:

My social horizons are expanding here in Isolation City. In one day, I met the remainder of my floormates (truly a rogues' gallery) at a party and also a very nice girl who works as my lab partner.

I met my across-the-hall neighbor quite by chance over a game of poker. I beat him over and over and he had to write me a few IOUs. When I asked him what room he was in (so I might stop by and "collect"), it turned out to be the room directly across from mine. It's weird how you can overlook someone who is right under your nose. Anyway, he's a nice guy, but is badly in need of tutoring in the finer points of the gentlemanly wager. He is absolutely the worst gambler I have ever encountered. I suspect that his brain has decomposed from excessive exposure to Jim, who is his favorite card player. They play to one another's caliber it seems. Two drunks leading each other home.

My neighbor's name is Marcum Standile, Jr. As a rather unusual point of insight into his personal life, we figured out tonight (in my room after the party) that Marcum owes roughly $40,000 to various other dormitory inhabitants with whom he has played poker. This sum is exceeded only by Jim's, whose debts accrued in two short months amount to a figure which is something akin to the annual budget for Red China. Perhaps my training in calculus is coming in handy for once.

I'll write more about Susie later. Everything is pretty good academically-speaking and the sun is, even, occasionally making a token appearance. Miss you very much and send all my love.

With endless computation,

P.S. Got a letter from you-know-who. Guess he took the accident a little too seriously. Tell him to relax.

April 4

Dear Mom and Dad:

I'm rich! Marcum got his monthly allotment from his financially overstuffed folks and came through with over $400 for yours truly. So far, this much money has me in quite an influential position since word of my monetary windfall has spread like an epidemic. I am popular beyond belief. I've considered opening up a loan service (with determined interest) so as to make the entire endeavor worth my expended energy as well as expended funds. An idea which I took from a movie with George Segal, "King Rat." The entire prison camp where he was being held captive by the enemy, had less money than George so he became the nucleus of all existing finance. The concept appeals to me. I'll probably just buy a heater and an electric blanket, though. Fancy dies so quickly in a young man's heart. Sniff.

I am referred to alternately as "Rockefeller" or "pal," depending on the plight of who I'm speaking with. I never dreamed any one person could have so many "pals." Last night someone pinned a sign to my door that says "Fort Knox North." It's only right. Being rich is such toil. Tell you-know-who I will use it wisely.

My lab partner and I have become even better friends in the past few weeks. I think I mentioned in the last letter that her name is Susie, actually Susan Johnson. What I failed to include in that brief description is that she is kind of like my girlfriend, stunningly beautiful, intelligent and popular and maybe the first girl, since Beth's death, that I really care about. Without pouring forth excessives about Susie, I'll simply say that I know you'd love her. She is quite a unique person and around here that's a godsend, the prevailing ambiance being composed of uptight females. I only hope that she feels the same about me. But that will come in time. I think it would crush me if she were just experiencing feelings of friendship. But I suspect that her eyes are the best spokesman for her affections and they tell me everything is going perfect. Tell you-know-who not to hold his breath. She isn't at all like Beth, so don't let him even attempt to connect things. Beth was just something that happened. I'm sorry about it, but it was, after all, an accident and I think I would resent you-know-who making more of this than there is. Or maybe making less of it. It feels right to me. Not like with Beth. So please keep you-know-who off the subject completely; it's not fair.

By the way, I think I might make the dean's list, so cross your fingers. Philosophy I is going very well and Marshall B. Francis and I are becoming friends of the close variety. As I predicted.

I miss you all very much and send my love. Please write.

With Krupp-like fortune,

P.S. Thanks for the latest batch of cookies, Mom. I'm not sure I can eat all of them myself. Plenty of willing mouths around here, though.

April 17
Dear Mom and Dad:

Terrible news. Remember Jim, the guy who belched and kept everybody up? He was found this morning, in his room, dead. The school won't issue any kind of statement, but everyone thinks it might have been suicide. I don't think there was a note or anything, and it could have just been an accident.

If it was suicide, it would have made a lot of sense, speaking strictly in terms of motivation. He wasn't a very happy person, his weight and all making him almost completely socially ostracized. He was only eighteen years old. It's a shame things like this have to happen.

It certainly is going to be quiet around here without his belching and carryings-on; which is kind of a relief even if the circumstances are so tragic. Nobody has mentioned the funeral but I hear his parents are going to have him buried locally. That's the nicest thing they could do for him. He really liked the college and the town and everything, and although unhappy, was happier here than he would have been anywhere else. It's going to be abnormally quiet around here. Maybe with the improved conditions we'll get some new scholars out of this dorm. I know I'll sleep better. Still, I feel as if every death has a meaning; a reason for happening. I may bring that up in Philosophy I. Anyway, it's a damn shame about Jim. Marcum lost a great card partner.

On a slightly cheerier note, Susie and I are still seeing each other, but I have a difficult time figuring her out. Maybe she isn't the demonstrative type. If that is the case, I can understand her reticence, but if not, I can't help wondering what's wrong. We talk all the time but she doesn't seem to be able to let me know she cares. It's odd because Beth was similar in that way.

I'm sure time will make its own decision. Sound familiar, Dad? It's another one of your polished "classics." What would life be without my father's inimitable cracker-barreling? A bit more relaxing perhaps...

Incidentally, the loan business is beginning to take shape. I'll write more about it later. For now, it's looking quite hopeful. Monte Carlo, here I come.

Pass the word to you-know-who, about my business. It's what he likes to hear. Former client makes good and all that stuff.

Miss you all very much and send my deepest love.

Destined to be wealthy
(but in semi-mourning),

P.S. My room is starting to bother me. Maybe a change!

April 25
Dear Mom and Dad:

You-know-who wrote me a letter I received today. He wants me to come home. The onslaught of Jim's death along with the isolating geography up here has him surprisingly alarmed. He feels that the milieu is just too strenuous for me to manage. I disagree with him completely and feel that I'm taking Jim's death very well. I'm not overreacting beyond what is reasonable. After all, Jim and I were almost complete strangers. Maybe the ease of detachment comes because of that.

I wrote you-know-who tonight after dinner, but I think a word from you might help to quell his skepticism. I know you told him about the death out of good conscience, but, as I recommended, it may have been a bad idea. All in all, I couldn't be happier and the thought of leaving depresses me very much. I think my letter will stand on its own merit, but a word from you would assist the cause enormously.

Business is in full swing here at Fort Knox North. I've made over $15 in interest this week. Once again, I'm baffled as to how to spend the newly mounting sums. Perhaps a place where liquor and painted women are available to book-weary students? However, I'll probably squander my gain away on decent food. The indigenous delicacies are becoming as palatable as boiled sheet metal. Really disgusting. I look forward to a meal by the greatest cook in the known world. I hope you're listening, Mom.

I talked to the dean of housing today about changing rooms and he told me (morbidly enough) that the only available room is Jim's. It seemed grisly at first, but I gave it serious thought and am going to move in tomorrow. It's been cleaned up (all but boiled out) so there is no trace of anything that indicated someone lived in it. Or died in it. For obvious reasons, I think you would agree, telling you-know-who would just fuel the flame. He can't expect everyone to react to death the same way. It doesn't spook me to be in Jim's room.

I wonder, though, if his spirit will inhabit my lungs and create zombie burps. All, no doubt, from your cookies, Mom. He was really hooked. Phantom gases are an interesting concept, but don't exactly arrest me esthetically. Quiet, I think I hear a cookie crumbling.

My studies are going exceptionally well. Something interesting happened in Philosophy I today. Remember I told you I was going to mention the point about Jim's death maybe being the happiest salvation he could have chosen? Well, I made the point and nobody would talk about it. They all seemed disturbed about the personalized nature of the question since it wasn't just a hypothetical inquiry. Some people even made peculiar comments. People are unpredictable when it comes to death.

Things are "OK" with Susie. We're supposed to go to a concert tonight. Will tell you about that in next letter. Miss you all hugely and send my fondest love.

Sleeping better,

P.S. Susie may get my class ring tonight. Lucky girl.

April 26
Dear Mom and Dad:

Something ghastly has happened. It's hard to even write this letter as I am extremely upset.

Susie and I returned from the school auditorium sometime after midnight, following the concert, and sneaked into my dormitory room to listen to some music. I had planned to ask Susie how she felt about me after we settled down. The concert had been very stimulating and we were both being quite verbal, competing for each other's audience as many thoughts were occurring to both of us. We talked for several hours and were almost exhausted from the conversation before quieting down.

As we sat listening to the music, on my bed together, I bent over to her cheek and, kissing her gently, asked her how she felt about our relationship and where it was going. She was silent for what must have been minutes. Then she spoke. In almost a pale whisper she said that we would always be good friends and that her regard for me was quite sincere but that she couldn't feel romantically about me ever. She didn't explain why, even though I asked her over and over.

Maybe the fact that I was tired had something to do with it, but I began to cry and couldn't stop. Her admission had taken me entirely by surprise. I had thought things were just beginning to take shape.

I guess Susie sensed that my hurt was larger than even the tears revealed and she got up from the bed to walk to the other side of the room. Working things out in her mind, I guess. She walked to the window to let in some air. As she raised it I could feel the cold wind rush in, and I looked up to see Susie's hair blowing as she kneeled near the window, looking out over the fields. It was so quiet that the whole thing seemed like a dream; the cold air plunging in on us, the music playing with muted beauty for us alone, the near darkness making shadowy nothings of our separateness.

Susie leaned out the window, and I watched her, transfixed, thinking that what she had said was a story, that she was only playing. She only continued in her silence, staring into the night's blackness.

I guess she wanted more air or something because she raised the window, and as I rose to help her with it, a screaming cut the air.

She kept screaming until she hit the walkway below. Then there was silence again. She was taken to the hospital and operated on for a fractured skull, broken shoulder, and internal injuries.

She was pronounced dead at 6:30 this morning.

The police questioned me today about the accident but seemed satisfied that it was a tragic accident. They could, I'm sure, see my grief was genuine.

I am left with almost nothing now. Susie was everything I worked for other than school, and without her here, that means nothing. I am thinking of coming home. You-know-who needn't say anything to you or me about what he thinks. He's wrong. And, at this point, I don't need advice. My treatment will be mine alone from now on. I don't want interference from him anymore.

I am very seriously depressed. I keep thinking that, had Susie told me long ago that she cared we wouldn't have spent so long, last night, in my room. If only she had cared, everything might have been different. I think these thoughts must occur to anyone who loses someone cherished. I didn't think something like this could happen to me. I find it hard to go on without someone caring. If you don't care about someone who cares about you, why should you even exist? Without that there is no reason.

In deepest hopelessness,

P.S. Maybe no letters from me until I feel better.

April 28
Dear Mom and Dad:

Things are no better with me than my last letter reported. Since Susie's death I am unable to concentrate on studies and am falling seriously behind in my classes. I sit alone most of the time in my room, watching the fields as the wind's create giant patterns. Before today, I had thought it the most beautiful view in the dorm.

Speaking of the dorm, I now find myself unable to associate with any of the other residents. They all remind me of Susie. I almost hate this building because it remembers everything that happened in it. It will not forget anything and each time I get inside it I feel subsumed by its creaking examinations of me. I am now easily given to imaginings about many things and question all things. I trust only myself now.

My loan business is being attended to assiduously with the scrutiny of a watchmaker fearing he has left out a part from a shipment of hundreds of timepieces. I am losing money now. The clientele is not paying me back punctually or with owed amounts adequately covered. Everybody on my floor and many people scattered throughout the building have taken out loans. Almost none have returned them. I am almost at my wit's end trying to get the money. But you can't torture people to get it. I'm really getting desperate. I have such contempt for those who borrow things and either refuse to return them or consciously allow themselves to let their obligation slide through negligence. Negligence should beget negligence. It's only fair that way.

I have been going to concerts the past two nights. They seem to help me relax. I despise returning to the dormitory more and more. Everytime I get inside I feel suffocated. I realize that I must try to adjust and get back into the swing of things, but it is not easy. I am trying. Tell you-know-who.

That's all I can tell you. I can't foresee much of anything now. My dearest love to both of you. Please write.

Confused with sickness,

April 30
Dear Mom and Dad:

Last night, almost as if the dormitory knew my hate for it (like a dog who senses its master's loathings), it took its own life along with the lives of many inside its cradling horror.

As I walked back from a 10:30 concert (Chopin) at the campus center, I came upon the dormitory burning bright orange in the night. Firemen say it was caused by an electrical short circuit or something. Nineteen students were eaten by flames, unable to escape the building. The remains were charred beyond recognition and teeth and dental records are being matched to discern who the students were.

It doesn't seem to matter who someone is once he is dead. Only what he did while he lived. An honorable life will not tolerate an impure death. But the life that deceives and cloaks its meaning with artifice and insensitivity cannot die reasonably. Perhaps Marshall B. Francis would have something to say about that. All death seems to need is an attached philosophy to resolve its meaning. Otherwise it is just an end. I may talk to him.

There is nothing left for me now of course. I am numbed by the death which surrounds me here. My room and belongings were destroyed in the fire, and the purpose of my schooling has become inconsequential to both myself and what I want.

I will try another school, in another place. Things must be different elsewhere. Somewhere there must be a safe place. A place where things such as what I have seen haven't happened. If there is, I will find it.

I'm catching a plane tomorrow at noon and should arrive at about 5:30. My love to you until then.

Forward looking,

P.S. I got an A in philosophy. Hooray!

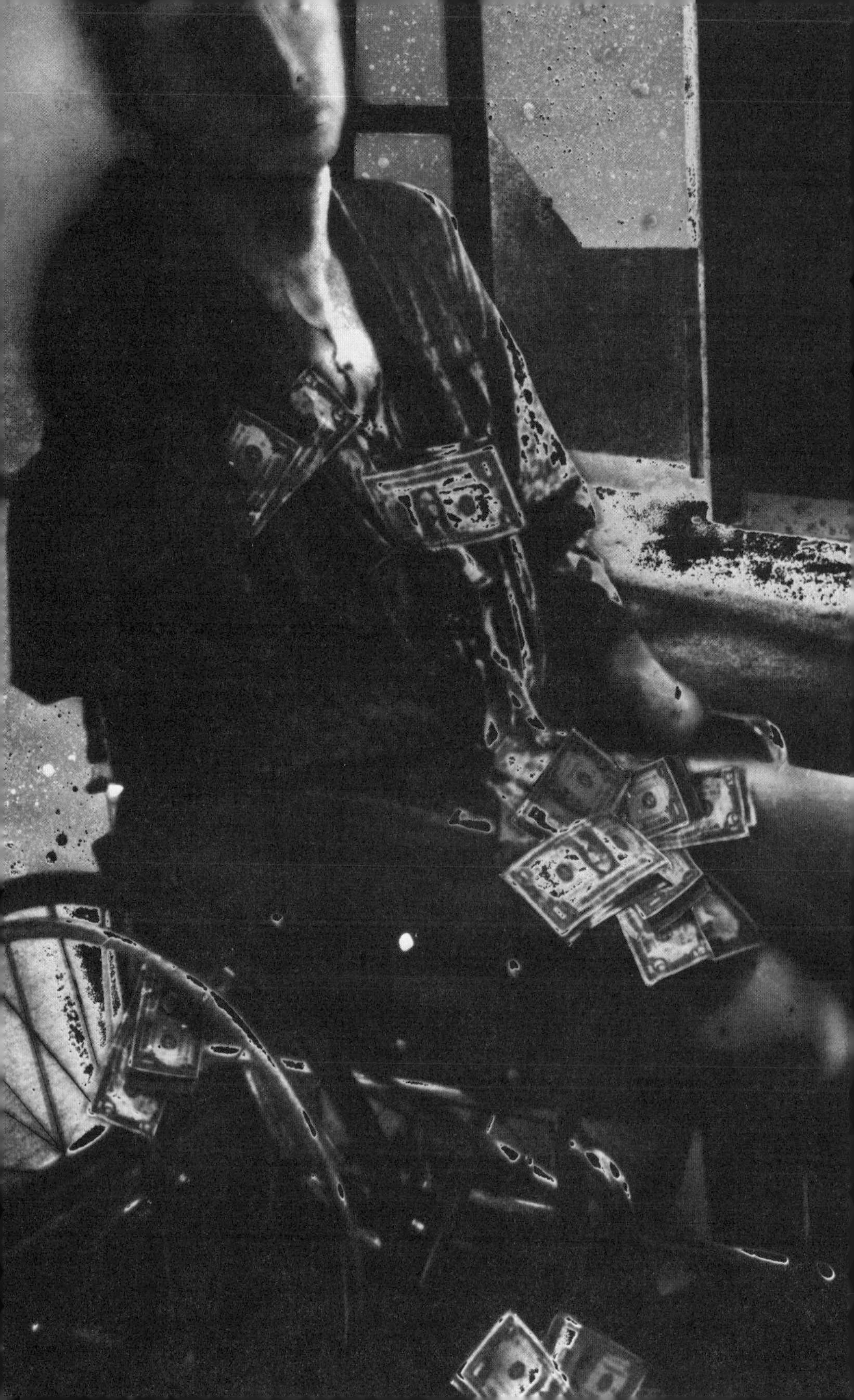

CONVERSATION PIECE

WHEN MY EDITOR first handed me the assignment, I said I wouldn't take it. Things like that had always turned my stomach. But I hadn't done a decent article in months and agreed to it.

I had expected the worst of grotesqueries when I pulled my car in front of the house. Finally after sitting for minutes, trying to fight the impulse to drive away, I went in.

The two of us sat in a small den and I was given coffee by the man's wife. As I sipped at the mug I turned on the tape recorder and began the interview.

Q. When did you first take a job offer?

A. After I graduated from college. I caught wind of the need from one of my professors.

Q. You received your degree in physical sciences, didn't you?

A. No. Anatomy. I was good at it. All it took was memorization.

Q. So, you spoke to one of your professors and he mentioned the need for volunteers. What did he say?

A. Not much. Only that the graduate medical studies program was doing a project and would I like to make some money.

Q. I would imagine that aspect of it sounded very appealing.

A. Extremely.

Q. Did they interview you? I mean I assume they had to be somewhat selective.

A. Oh, sure. Mainly they check for physical health. In the majority of their experiments they're checking for the impact of viral introduction on healthy tissue.

Q. And you checked out?

A. Perfectly. Which is amazing. Between the hours I was keeping and the lousy food I was eating you'd think I would have been anemic or something.

Q. You must have a strong constitution.

A. Guess so. Damned if I can figure it.

Q. So what was your first assignment?

A. It's been a long time but I can still remember it.

Q. How many years back was that?

A. Nineteen.

Q. You look younger than that.

A. (*laughs*) Thank you.

Q. You were saying . . .

A. Well, what they wanted from me was just a little blood. They were doing leukemia research. So I gave a couple pints and they made out a check.

Q. What'd they pay you?

A. I don't even remember. Back in those days it wasn't much, of course. But I do remember cashing that first check and taking my girl out.

Q. Did it bother this girl? The way you were making your money?

A. Not at first.

Q. I don't understand that answer.

A. Well, for the first year it was pretty innocent. You know, blood, sleep deprivation, alcohol studies. Temporary stuff.

Q. That changed?

A. *Absolutely.*

Q. How soon after you'd started?

A. The third year.

Q. Why then?

A. This girl I mentioned, she wanted to get married. That's what started the problem.

Q. How so?

A. Well, her folks didn't approve of me, so I had to pick up the tab for everything.

Q. What did you do?

A. Well, I was stuck. So I went to this clinic and let a doctor take a skin biopsy from underneath my chin. I only got paid fifty dollars but it paid for the minister and it got my foot in the door.

Q. Got your foot in the door?

A. Sure. This doctor, he spread the word that I was available and that I was good.

Q. What determines how good you are?

A. Well, like we were saying before, health counts for everything. But after that, attitude is what separates the fringe elements from the professionals.

Q. What is different about your attitude?

A. Well, I try and get involved in the experiment. Some guys, they just come in and do what they're told without putting out any effort. To me, the experiment is something to be taken seriously. Believe me, that outlook was appreciated and it got me a lot of work.

Q. What did you do after the wedding? Did you continue to use your body to make money?

A. I tried not to. I tried different jobs. I worked as a printer's assistant, as a librarian, a liquor store delivery boy. But none of them really appealed to me. I never liked work much. Maybe that's why selling parts of my body was so easy for me. There was no work involved.

Q. Just pain?

A. A little. I learned to accept it.

Q. It seems that would have discouraged you.

A. In some odd way it seemed to add to it. As if I needed punishment for my laziness. Or maybe for my lack of happiness with my wife.

Q. There were marital problems?

A. We argued constantly. She hated my work.

Q. You told her about it?

A. No, but she caught on. It showed. I couldn't very well hide the scars and stitches. My body betrayed me.

Q. What was her reaction?

A. She was disgusted. Revolted by my gradual deterioration. Yet she admitted we needed the money.

Q. (*checking notes*) I read here that you were nearly divorced. What happened? Was there a breaking point?

A. Yes. It's funny, she could allow herself to deal with my selling certain parts of my body but not others. To sell a vial of my bone marrow was tolerable. To let them buy a lung or a finger or an ear was tolerable. But when we were expecting a child, we needed money again, and I sold my hands.

Q. What in particular about that bothered her?

A. She said the stumps of my arms on her back, with only the cauterized wrists touching her, gave her nightmares. But our baby had the best. I did whatever I had to do. I was taking care of my family. What man wouldn't do the same?

Q. After you had your hands taken off, did she leave you?

A. Mentally, yes. She wouldn't have much to do with me. We slept in separate beds, practically didn't talk. Occasionally she'd hand me my baby daughter and expect me to rock her. I loved that. I'd rock her to sleep in my arms. I really felt like a father.

Q. I guess every parent reacts that way.

A. I'm sure. But it didn't last long. The baby got sick and needed special medicine. I had to go to work again. I had to sell my arms and some fluid from my nervous system. I made a lot that time.

Q. *(waiting for a moment)* You were going to talk about the marriage.

A. Yes. I got off the track. When our daughter entered grade school she needed clothes, so I went to work again. The bills were coming in fast and steady. I was forced to sell some of my internal organs and a large skin patch from my scalp.

Q. What about your hair?

A. I'd sold that months before. It gave me a down payment on a washer.

Q. Didn't you ever want to just stop and get into some other profession?

A. No, like I said, I really enjoy this type of work. Besides it was getting to the point where I couldn't have done anything else.

Q. How so?

A. Well, by that time I'd sold my legs to a clinic doing research in limb restoration and wasn't able to get around without help.

Q. Did your wife help you to go to your jobs?

A. Yes, she became better about it over time. I guess every marriage has a period of adjustment.

Q. And your daughter?

A. Such a beautiful little girl. She's in the second grade now.

Q. So, how have you been getting along lately?

A. Pretty well. I've got a few things lined up.

Q. You think you can keep going?

A. Oh, sure. I've got lots of good years ahead of me. The marriage is getting better and I'm very satisfied with my work.

Q. But you have so little left.

A. (*laughs a little*) You'd be surprised how much there still is. My chin is healing. I'll be able to start selling biopsy plugs from there soon. And I hear of this doctor who is doing work in the dental nerve responses. Hell that could give me thirty-two jobs if I played it right.

Q. You're not worried?

A. Not at all. I can still sell my brain tissue, or my eyelids.

Q. But what will you do when ... everything's gone?

A. Oh, that won't be for a long, long time. And besides, as far as money goes I've got some tucked away and I've been getting my wife a few jobs. For instance, day before yesterday she did some muscle exertion experiments. Got paid fifty dollars.

Q. You don't think she might ...

A. Can't tell yet. It's too early. But she'd be good, and the money's very good.

Q. Keep it in the family.

A. Sort of. I could show her a lot. Who knows, maybe even my daughter. I understand there's a big need for certain brain fluids that can only be gotten from a child.

Q. That wouldn't bother your conscience?

A. A little.

Q. I'd like to ask you one last question. What do you think of what you are doing? Morally, I mean.

A. Morally? ... well, that's a good question. I've never really thought about it. But I suppose it's kind of like this. The world has lots of progress to make and it's people like myself and now maybe my wife and daughter who make it possible. We are the people of tomorrow, in a romantic sense. Without us, others would have no chance.

I turned off my tape recorder and got my things together.

One year after the article came out, I heard from his wife that he'd died. Except it wasn't really like a death. There was just nothing left.

Even now, at times, I play that interview tape late at night and remember how happy he looked as he spoke. With no body, and patches of raw skin covering his face, scalp and neck. For something as horrible as he was, he seemed to have no regrets. Perhaps in some way, the more he gave up the more he felt he had.

Sometimes, with all my pressures I can't help but feel that I'm losing parts of myself. A little at a time. A conviction here, an honesty there. It adds up. And you know, I really can't be sure anymore if I'm less crazy than he was.

StateNational

ECHOES

LUPO WAS IN HIS HUGE OFFICE sipping coffee and going over contracts when a sound of crying leaked into the room from the distance. It startled him and he moved to his window, looking out as the voice pleaded for someone to take away the pain. Sixteen stories below, the tangles of mid-town traffic moved in tiny patterns, horns blasting ant noise. But it wasn't the sound.

He closed his eyes, concentrating harder on the direction the noise was coming from, as the wind clawed his building, sideswiping the mirrored surface with a muted whine. But it was a different sound; not the one he heard.

His expression darkened as he began to wander his office and the weeping continued; misery worsening. He turned left and right, trying to pinpoint its source but heard only the faraway clacking of typewriters as secretaries sprayed words on paper, outside his door.

He shook his head and lit a cigarette.

Bizarre. Hearing things. What next? Guys in the drool wagon coming to cart him away?

He was about to head out of his office and recruit a second opinion when the crying suddenly vanished; gone as quickly as it started. The groans which rose and fell, underscoring the helplessness were gone, too.

All of it simply stopped.

He let go of the doorknob and took a deep drag on his Winston, holding the smoke in his lungs, waiting.

Nothing changed. He was in his office on a Monday morning, going over contracts and everything was well and normal. He waited for two minutes. Three. Crushed his cigarette out and smiled. Whatever the hell it was, it was done with. Maybe he'd better start getting more sleep, not working out so hard at the club. Pass on the blow. He remembered what his doctor had said about successful executives in their forties. Had to watch it. Stressola, buddy. Nobody came with a warranty.

He walked back to his desk to finish his coffee but stumbled halfway.

A woman's tortured shriek exploded in his head. And with each passing second, the scream multiplied, growing to hundreds, then thousands, as if some audible cancer. But now there were different voices. Children's. Men's. Old voices. Young. All calling out in helpless suffering. It sounded as if the entire world had gone mad inside his head and Lupo slapped his hands over his ears, feeling like throwing up.

But the dread chorus only got louder, the infinite voices continuing to bellow their anguish. His face went white and he tried to reach for his intercom... his secretary could call an ambulance. Get him to a hospital. Some kind of sedative. A shot. They could cut his head open and take the noise out... God, he was losing his mind.

The howling voices grew still louder, calling out like tormented animals and Lupo's fingernails dug into his palms, causing blood to drip. He tried to yell, tried to move. But he had fallen to the floor and his entire body drew into itself, shuddering. Then, without him feeling it happen, his mouth contorted into a monstrous opening and a hideous sound climbed his throat. But he couldn't hear it as it burst from his mouth. His screams were only one tiny voice in the millions as he lurched toward the window.

* * *

MILLIONAIRE EXECUTIVE
PLUNGES FORTY FLOORS

No Motive Evident In
Strange Death Of
Arms Manufacturer

INCORPORATION

THE BLACK ROLLS passed through the gate, winding its way through the grounds of the estate, and parked before the immense mansion.

The driver came around, opened the door and Joel slid from the leather seat.

"He's waiting," advised the driver.

Joel nodded and approached the mansion's imposing front door. After all this time, why would Longstreet want to talk to him he wondered? He'd always done well for the old man's corporations. A good company man, thought Joel. That's me. So what on earth did Longstreet have in mind? He lifted the brass knocker on the front door and it came down with a rich thud.

After a moment, the door slowly opened and a tall butler with a dour face stood looking down at Joel.

"Please come in."

Joel passed through the doorway with an uneasy smile and stood in the entryway of the enormous mansion. All around him loomed statuary and classic paintings. Tapestries and chandeliers hung in silence. A home of wealth, thought Joel, eyeing it all. Unbelievable wealth.

"Mr. Longstreet is waiting for you in the library," said the butler, gesturing with open palm toward a door down the main hall.

Joel walked behind the butler and absently reached to straighten his own tie and vest. He cleared his throat once and the butler turned a bit looking at Joel, over his shoulder. Joel tried to not look apologetic.

"Through here, sir," said the austere servant, directing Joel to the half-open door.

Joel smiled thanks, which was not returned, and quietly knocked on the door.

"Come in," answered a commanding voice from within.

Inside, he was met by a beautifully panelled room with a roaring fireplace at one end and books covering three walls. Standing before the fireplace was Longstreet. Sixty-five and handsome as a movie star.

"Joel. I'm pleased you could keep our date."

"Wouldn't have missed it, sir," said Joel shaking Longstreet's hand. But missed just exactly *what*, he wondered.

"Drink?" offered Longstreet.

"Great," said Joel, noticing the monogram on Longstreet's silk dinner jacket: HML. Horatio Miles Longstreet. He remembered the full name from that first meeting, when Longstreet had hired him for his international sales division. It was only one of Longstreet's many corporations but he could still remember his excitement. Working as a young executive for H.M. Longstreet.

The richest man in the world.

Longstreet handed Joel a crystal snifter.

"Brandy alright?"

"Perfectly," answered Joel, relaxing a bit at the cordiality.

"Joel," said Longstreet, "I've brought you up here so we'd have an opportunity to talk, free of the distractions of the office."

Joel breathed the aroma of the brandy, holding the snifter close to his nose. He nodded as Longstreet spoke, listening attentively to the older man's words.

"I've been watching you, you know," said Longstreet, looking at Joel.

"Watching?"

"And observing," said Longstreet, moving to the fireplace and reaching in with a poker to stir the hot logs. "I think your work with the corporation has been absolutely first rate."

Joel brightened visibly.

"Well, Mr. Longstreet, that's wonderful." He was unable to restrain a sincere smile.

"For both of us, Joel. You see, I'd like to talk about your future with me."

"You sir?"

"Well, I mean my business, of course. But then, I am my business, after all, aren't I?"

Joel smiled at the comment.

Longstreet laughed and Joel took another sip of brandy, his impatience driving him crazy. This was it and he knew it. Longstreet was getting at something big. Very big.

"I think it's time we got down to specifics," suggested Longstreet as Joel's ears perked, "I want to incorporate you into my inner circle of executives."

He patted Joel on the shoulder and walked over toward the bar. "Refill?"

"Thank you," said Joel, trying to mask his astonishment as Longstreet poured another brandy. This was turning out to be more than just a simple raise or promotion.

Longstreet was offering to incorporate him into the whole thing. Straight to the top.

"Come, I'll explain further," said Longstreet, opening the door.

Joel followed behind, his insides frothing with excitement. Was Longstreet kidding? Had Joel done that fabulous a job? He remembered the sales pushing up when he joined on. Winning the annual award for most outstanding division manager. But ... this was a total shock.

The two men entered the den off the library in which another fireplace blazed cozily. Hung throughout the room were several portrait-sized paintings of young men dressed in conservative jacket, vest and tie, all projecting vitality and determination.

"Other young men in my organization who have been incorporated into the business," said Longstreet, anticipating Joel's question. He waited for Joel to say something.

"I'm deeply flattered, Mr. Longstreet. But I must confess I wasn't prepared for this offer." Joel shook his head, impressed. "I'm stunned, sir."

"Why? You're young, intelligent, gifted in business, ambitious. A leader. All the things I admire most in a man. The things that make me want to incorporate any young man into my business."

As Longstreet spoke, Joel was suddenly swept by a leaden density, and his eyes lost focus.

"What will my new post be?" he asked, struggling to concentrate through dizziness.

"Why, none," answered Longstreet, watching Joel carefully.

Joel's legs started to fold.

"But you said you wanted to incor ... " he couldn't finish and moved to a thickly tufted chair, collapsing into it.

Longstreet moved closer.

"That's right," he said, "I do. I think it makes me stronger as an executive to have young men in the center of my business. But you forget what I said before, Joel."

Longstreet moved to the fireplace and pushed a button which activated an immense, motorized spit suspended above the crackling logs. It groaned as it began to turn, large enough to hold a sizable animal.

Weak and near unconsciousness, Joel looked up to see Longstreet looking at him with a voracious stare, waiting for the drug to take effect.

"I *am* my business."

HELL

August. Two-thirteen a.m.

L.A. was turning on a spit and teenagers were out in cars everywhere, cooking alive, tortured. The insanity of summer's sauna made the city grow wet and irritable, and blood bubbled at a sluggish boil in the flesh. Animals slept deeply, too hot to move, fur smelling of moist lethargy. Chewing gum came to life on sidewalks, like one-celled creatures, growing in the heat and the glow of fires created arsonist sunsets on the foothills which rimmed the city.

LAUREN PULLED her VW Rabbit into the view area off Mulholland, damp hair sticking to her forehead in fang shapes. The Rabbit rolled against the concrete headstone at the parking slot's end that prevented berserkos from driving over the edge and she killed the engine. Hollywood was spread before her, eating electricity, *hibachi*-bright. To her side, in the two other parked cars, she saw silhouette couples, in back seats, groping, fucking; glistening under the swelter.

Her skull was slowly steaming open and she punched on the AM-FM as insects broiled on her radiator like tiny steaks. She tuned in a station and a moody deejay came-to over the airwaves, laughing softly like a rapist. Lauren was numb from the burning night and rolled down her window more, letting in the oven.

"Here's a track the needle *loves* to lick." He made a faint licking noise. Laughed more, soft and cruel. "Mick and the boys given' us some sympathy for a bad man. In case you're wonderin' about L.A.'s needle ...it's in the red, babies. Hundred and two in the dark. I feel hot...How 'bout you?"

He chuckled as if tying a woman up and lowering onto her terrified body. Then "Sympathy For the Devil" 's rhythmic trance began and Lauren leaned back, staring out the windshield, sweat glazing her forehead. Hot wind blew air that felt sour and old and smog stuck to everything. They called it, riot weather after the Watts riots back in the Sixties.

Bad wind. Poison days.

She rubbed her eyes and remembered the heat and humidity of that kerosene summer a million years ago. It had put a blister on top of L.A. and all those welfare cases cooking-up in their crackerbox hells went insane. Killed. Looted. Shoved broken glass into cop's throats and watched them bleed to death for fun. People said it was the thermometer that finally triggered it. Just a hot, wet summer day that made people itch and drink and lose their tempers and carve each other up for relief.

She tapped tiredly on the wheel, following Jagger's voice as it stabbed, pulled the knife out and stabbed again. Ran fingers through sweat-salted hair, feeling as if she'd taken her clothes out of a dryer half-wet and put them on.

The song thinned to nothing and the deejay was groaning, sounding like it was all over and he needed a cigarette. She wiped her forehead, starting to feel sick from the heat which crept in her windows. She unbuttoned her blouse lower, inviting what breeze hadn't been baked solid and felt her mouth parting, her breathing slow. The two cars beside hers started and pulled away, leaving her surrounded by shapes the exhaust formed under moonlight.

The deejay came out of a commercial for a de-tox clinic and hissed lewd amusement.

"Hope you're with the one who makes you get *hideous* out there." He paused and Lauren could see him grinning cynically like a psycho killer in a courtroom, enjoying the grotesque evidence. "Temperature ... a hundred and two and a half. How 'bout some Doors? 'Back Door Man,' summer of '69. Where were you?" Sensual, torturer's breathing. "And ... who were you tormenting?"

The night felt suddenly swampier as requiem notes hit the air and Lauren closed her eyes, spinning, sweating, feeling creeks of perspiration run down her ribs. She drifted farther, remembering a beach party in August of '69 when she'd taken her first acid trip and glided for eight hours in a Disney borealis, able to listen to handfuls of sand that spoke to her in frantic whispers. What was it it had said? She tried to remember ... something about mankind suffering. Hating itself. It had terrified her.

She opened her eyes trying to forget, as another car pulled into the slot beside hers—a teenage, muscle cruiser; primered, deafening. Heavy Metal howled and though the windows were tinted, she could see cigarette tips roving inside, as whoever drove watched the city.

She wiped sweat which slid between her breasts and watched two other cars racing closer, up Mulholland, headlights jabbing; hunting. The cars finally prowled into the view area, one beside her, one behind. She felt massive engines shaking the pavement and the cars on either side were so close she realized she couldn't open her doors. The new cars beside her, on the right, had tinted windows like the one on the left. Inside the new one, she saw cigarettes, maybe joints, making slow moving graffiti patterns. Heard muted laughter; unsettling voices. Male and female.

Restless.

She tried her doors and neither would open; blocked.

The deejay sighed depressively. "Another knifing downtown. Simply Blues Bar." A yawn. The sound of something icy and long being swallowed. "Some people just shouldn't drink. Let's get back to the Doors."

Lauren pushed harder on her driver's door that felt fused shut. There was no play in it and she yelled to the driver to move his car. But there was no answer and when she did the same on the other side, still nothing. As she knocked sweating hands on the windows of both cars, Morrison started screaming.

"... well the music is your only friend.
Dance on fire as it intends.
Music is your only friend. Until the end."

Lauren gave up on the cars which blocked her doors, started the Rabbit, jammed it into reverse, hit the gas and let out the clutch. Her tires gushed sticky, black dust but the car behind her didn't move. She started to panic, unable to escape and screamed at the drivers pressing against her, on three sides, to move their cars. She caught her expression in the Rabbit's rearview; a fleeting look of terror.

"The face in the mirror won't stop,
the girl in the window won't drop.
A feast of friends—'Alive!' she cried.
Waiting for me outside. Outside!"

She pounded harder on the windows of both cars but no one responded. Just more murmured amusement behind tinted glass. Cigarette tips burning, shifting like creature eyes. She slid across the front seat again, grunting trapped, primitive sounds and banged on the tinted windows of the opposite car. She could see her helpless features reflected in the black glass and gripped the door more tightly as she screamed.

"Before I sink
into the big sleep.
I want to hear the scream
of the butterfly."

The Doors kicked her harder and her hands began to bruise from pounding the glass; yellow-purple flesh replacing pink. Her throat was grated by screams and though she couldn't make out voices, the laughter in the surrounding cars grew louder. She began to cry and the deejay chuckled.

"Just stepped outside and the flames are rising. Don't forget to use your lotion guys and gals." He made an obscene squirting sound. "Quick thought for the night: maybe we're all cooking alive and don't know it ... so, let's party."

He killed the Doors and substituted demented music which started suddenly, making Lauren's heart beat too fast.

She immediately looked up when the car behind hers began to rumble like a piece of earth moving equipment and started forward, shoving the Rabbit's front tires over the cement block. Then, the rear tires. It pushed harder, engine screaming, tires spinning. Ahead, the sequin sea of L.A. glittered.

Lauren tried frantically to get out her doors but the other cars rolled over their own cement blocks and stopped her, jamming either side like grisly escorts.

She looked ahead, saw the cliff's edge and grabbed the wheel tightly, trying to lock the tires. But the Rabbit kept sliding closer to the edge, tires gouging fat scars in the dirt. She held down the horn, trying to let someone know, then covered her face with both hands, plunging into blackness; a burning spray twisting end over end. Her scream lasted seconds.

As the three cars drove away into the muggy gloom the deejay made a sound of exquisite pain. "Another ghastly evening in the City of Angels. In case you're keeping score, the temperature just went up another degree ...and you're *losing*." The six headlights stared around a curve and disappeared, looking for places to go; things to do. Sirens wailed and moved toward Mulholland as the deejay blew smoke into the mike, spun a ballad and cooed Aushwitz delight. "Stay bad, babies ...the night is young. And there's no way out."

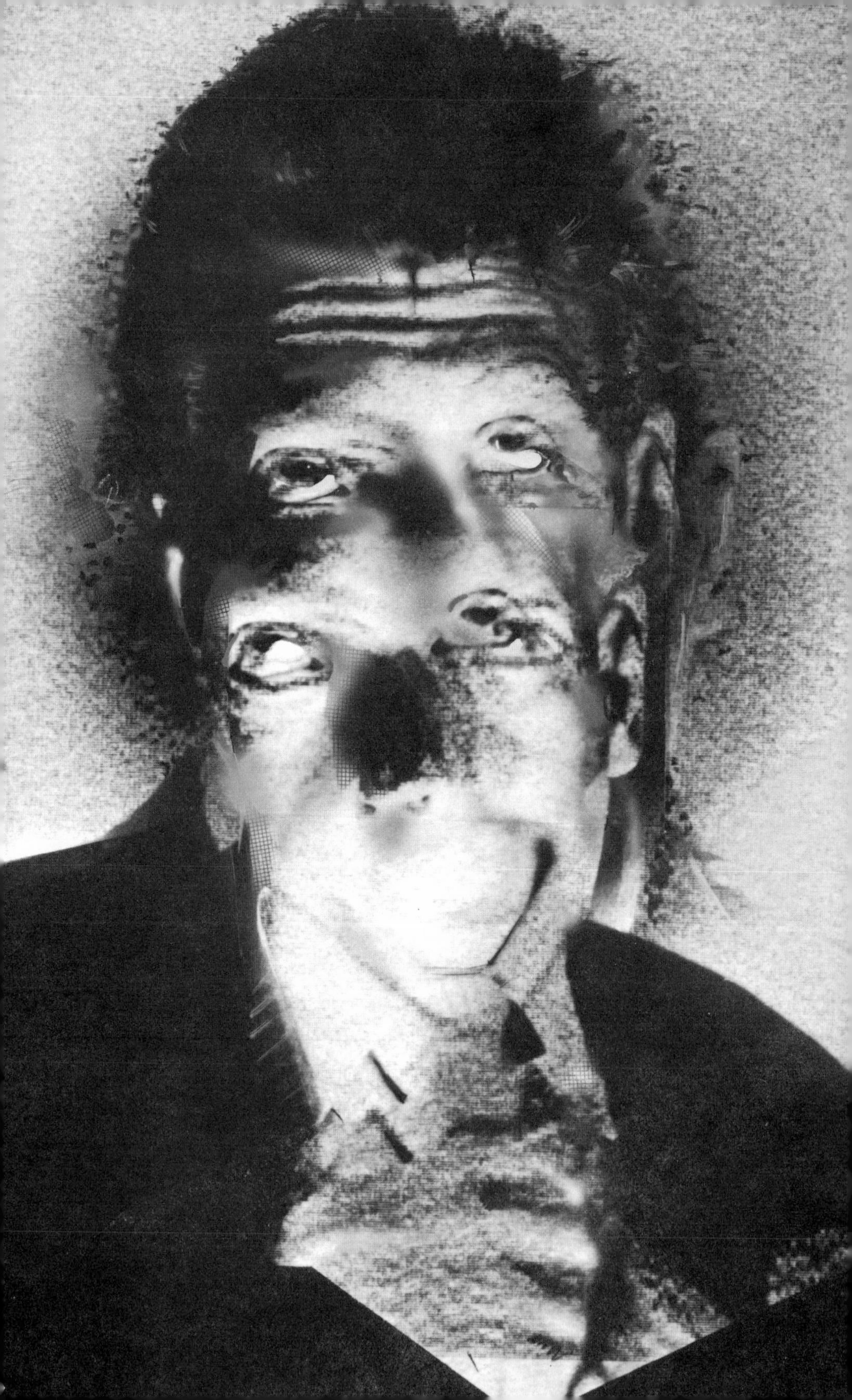

BREAK-UP

THEY WERE IN BED, curled together like children. That was when he whispered it and her expression quietly tore open. She asked how long he'd felt this way. He gestured without detail and guessed two or three weeks. She stared at him, wanting to know how soon he intended to break things off.

"Now," he answered, a silhouette.

She gathered the comforter around herself like a funeral shroud and started to cry when he told her the relationship was good but that for reasons he couldn't name, he wanted out.

"I'll change," she offered, sitting higher, ready to negotiate. She grasped a glass of water from her bedside table with pale fingers and told him she could be more what he wanted. She'd find a way. She watched for his reaction, optimism trapping her.

He rose and began to dress, telling her it was too late. He needed something different. But even as he said it, in some odd sense he didn't relate to the words. Still, he made no effort to correct the message, though it frightened him.

She tried to understand and told him if he needed time off, to take as much as he required. A weekend. A year. She would wait.

He began buttoning his shirt, tying his tie. She watched as he laced his wing-tips and asked if he would call.

"...no." He wouldn't say more.

"You can't do this to us!" Her eyes were wide, angry. He was an executioner, sentencing them.

He pulled on his suit coat, sat on the bedside, spoke softly.

"Try to understand. It's not us. It's me. People grow. They want different things. Nothing's forever." He didn't know where the ideas were coming from and felt himself in some grotesque trance.

Sun struck the brass headboard, as if controlled by a catwalk technician and lit her bloodless lips. They parted to free a sound of drowning; assassination. "It's someone else, isn't it?"

"No. I'm just feeling different from when we met." He tried to remember when or how they'd met and couldn't. He felt sick.

"We've known each other six months and you've already fallen out of love? What about all the promises? Our plans? *Damn* you!" She tried to slap him but thoughtlessly drew her fingers into claws and swiped his skin. Three uneven scratches etched war-paint stripes under one eye and he wiped his cheek, smearing a cuff red. He tried to say something as she watched the blood glide down his face.

"I'm sorry, Jill ...maybe you're right, maybe I don't love you anymore ...I don't know. If I could explain it ..." he sounded lost; unable to translate himself. "...I just have to move on."

She looked poisoned. "Get out. *Now.*"

He grabbed his wallet and keys, looked at her one last time and closed the door behind himself. She caught her reflection in the mirror and threw the bedside clock at her deserted image.

Outside her apartment, he walked toward his car and stopped to lean against the wall in the underground garage. He was suddenly nauseous and a spasm broke glass in his stomach. He began to vomit and as he arched over the greasy cement, the sensation felt somehow familiar, the pains like dim memories. He became more sick and tried to think about the conversation he'd just had with ...but he couldn't recall her name.

Or who she was. Or what they'd been doing.

He stared down at his right hand, which supported him against the wall as he coughed. But he no longer recognized it;

where it had been slight of structure, covered with fine, blond fuzz, it now had black hair on its back and knuckles. The wrists were growing thicker, fingers more powerful, tendons sleek beneath the now tanned skin. He tried to concentrate on where he was and saw an I.D. bracelet on his wrist. It grew gradually more tight and he unclasped it. On one side was an engraving:

"I Love You, *Madly.* Jill."

He stared at it, thinking, concentrating, unable to place the name. He flipped it and on the other side was another name: *David*. He felt a flicker of recollection but it vanished in seconds and he was quickly distracted by the feeling of growing taller, more sinewed. He felt an aggressive stream of ideas and sensations filling his mind; things deep inside dying, other things replacing them, taking over, taking control. He sensed he'd been through this hundreds of times, somehow even knew it, as the change spread like a perverse warmth, becoming more potent, settling within his cells; becoming them.

He stopped vomiting. Stood straight.

He was inches taller, pounds heavier. His face had broadened, the nose more flat. A heavy stubble had come in and he felt his face, probing at the red wounds on his cheek as they filled in and closed. He ran strong hands through hair that was now long and curly as a woman came up behind him.

"Excuse me? I'm looking for my boyfriend?"

He turned and Jill stared at him, hoping he could help. But he didn't remember anything about her and in a deep voice said he'd seen no one. Then he walked away, not knowing to take his car. As he exited the garage and moved down the street, he felt a wallet against his thigh, withdrew it. He looked at the face on the driver's license and felt nothing as he bellowed the wallet wide, took the cash and tossed it aside.

Then, feeling the morning sun on his new life, he walked on, good for another six months.

MR. RIGHT

THE YOUNG WOMAN wept, "He's such an absolute bastard, doctor. He does the most horrible things."

The doctor shifted in the chair and continued to take notes. "What made you decide to come in and talk?"

The woman hesitated.

"Because he's gotten worse," she said, "Last night he asked me to fix him something to eat." Her mouth pulled downward, "He had me heat the stew until it was burning hot then suddenly got angry about something."

The woman's voice began to shudder.

"Before I could protect myself, he grabbed my hands and held them over the stove. She held up raw palms, covered with salve.

The doctor cringed a little, "Did you call the police?"

"No. He yanked the phone out of the wall, then he beat me with his belt." She rubbed at her arms. "My whole body is covered with welts."

"How long has this been going on?" the doctor asked.

The woman gestured shakily.

"I can't remember. Three years. Maybe more."

"Have you tried to leave him?"

"Everyday," the woman answered, trying to steady herself, "But he finds me. I try to turn him away but what he does to me in bed..."

The doctor looked up from the notes. "Can you be more specific? It's important that I understand what you're going through. It's the first step in a successful treatment."

The woman looked at the doctor uneasily.

"Last night..."

"Yes...?"

"...last night, after he beat me up, he tied me to the bedposts in my bedroom." She drew shallow breath, "Then he raped me."

The doctor swallowed.

"It was horrible but at the same time it was wonderful. He does things like I've never had any man do." For the first time, the woman showed signs of a smile. "Incredible things. Like a fantasy come true."

The doctor jotted notes. "Can you describe the things he does?"

The woman fell into uncomfortable silence.

"I couldn't, it's so intimate. I just couldn't."

The doctor nodded, "When you're ready."

Unexpectedly, the woman's face tensed.

"Doctor, I'm so scared. He's so crazy and I can't make myself pull away."

The doctor made a sympathetic sound and continued to listen.

"He's killed two of my dogs and last week he killed an entire litter of my cat's kittens with a knife." The woman's eyes shut tightly. "When he was a boy, he battered a rabbit to death with a hammer. And he's done even more horrible things. He's told me."

Was there no *end?* thought the doctor.

"He tried to poison a friend of mine because she kept begging him to sleep with her and bothering him." The woman's cheekbones quivered. "He sent her candies and signed the card from her children. They were filled with arsenic. She's dying right now." The woman held her head. "Nerve damage."

The doctor set the note pad on the desk.

"Listen to me. You must leave this man, immediately. *Today.*"

"But he makes me feel things that no man has. Maybe if I compromise. Maybe you could talk to him."

"No. I'll call him for you," the doctor said, "but I'll lie. I'll tell him that I've had you moved to a hospital in another part of the country. I want you on a plane today."

The doctor touched the woman's hand.

"You *must* escape him. There's no room for compromise. This man is sick. He shouldn't be allowed around sane people."

The woman tightened her grasp on the doctor's hand like a child seeking protection. "You don't think that what he makes me feel in bed is the truth?" she asked, "Maybe he really *does* love me?"

The doctor shook the woman's hand, insistently.

"*No!* You must believe me. Your time may be running out."

"Other women have responded in the same way," the woman continued, as if to justify her plight. "He brings them all to ecstasy."

The doctor pressed a buzzer on the desk and interrupted the woman, who was beginning to cry again. "I want you to make a one-way reservation to Honolulu," the doctor told the secretary. "In Miss Shubert's name...for today."

The doctor took hold of the woman's shoulders.

"Now listen to me. I want you to go home and pack, take a cab to the airport and leave today. Call me when you get there. It's the only way you'll survive this maniac."

The woman looked up at the doctor with defenseless eyes and nodded.

"Good," said the doctor.

Fifteen minutes after Miss Shubert's flight had taken off, the doctor sat overlooking the city, completing notes. The buzzer sounded on one of the phone extensions and the doctor pushed down the lit button.

"Yes? This is Miss Shubert's psychiatrist," said the doctor. "No, I don't know where she is. She left today without a word. But I'm glad I reached you. I think you're somebody I'd really like to get to know."

The doctor trembled, running hands through her own hair, imagining the first thing he'd do to her.

CANCELLED

ZZZZ...(cough)...zzz...Jesus Christ! (cough cough)... throat's dry as the friggin' Sudan. What time is it? (cough) Four-thirty...God...my tongue feels like the inside of friggin' Graceland; a coat of velveteen crud.

God. Damned party went on forever. All those network putzes talkin' their pilots....Jesus. Love being a producer. Like livin' in a friggin' Gucci leper colony. Okay, head into the kitchen and grab a bottle of belch juice. Left, right, left, right...yawn. Christ...my head's a goddamned banana republic. That's what you get, pal. Keep better hours. Keep telling you. Yow! Kitchen floor. Italian tiles cold as a goddamn ice-rink.

Jesus H.

Okay...open-friggin'-sesame to the fridge and grab that little Parisian dew-drop container. Whoosh that sucker open. Tilt the brain box. Look out stomach. Oh, God.

Much better. Thank God for water with bubbles from France. Have kibbutz-sized ulcers like Marty, otherwise. So screw him. Deserves every one. Worst agent ever slithered from the bile. Couldn't sell free money with a loaded gun. May he drown in all the blood he sucks, including mine. Friggin' maggot.

Okay. Bottle in the trash and a quick belcherooney!

Oh, yeah.

Back into the bedroom, passing the marble table from the ex. Total nightmare; looks like a friggin' sacrificial slab. Appropriate, n'est-ce pas? Only thing I got after the settlement. May she burn up along with the Radcliffe lard she jogs off at that $5,000-a-week health camp in Hungaria.

Hey, the trades sitting on top of her slab. Goddammit, Sam's new horror flick, *Garbage Disposal Weekend*, is smack on the cover of *Variety*. Doing boffo b.o. it says. So get a better deodorant, Sam.

Christ, that inane sonofabitch couldn't write if he was a pencil.... *Garbage Disposal Weekend*. Real class, Sam. Why not *Pus Weekend*? Too tame? How about *Cannibal Pope*? You putz. And direct? Sure, Sam, you can direct. Oh, yeah. And friggin' monkeys wear pants and smoke Panatellas. Fraudulent sonofabitch. Why don't you hop in that boffo b.o. bloody garbage disposal of yours and put yourself on puree? Ripped me off last season on that *Krishna Squad* movie of the week and you know it.

Belch...

Karma, Sam, karma. May you come back in your next life as a Xerox machine. Prick.

Okay, pal, back into the bedroom and get some friggin' sleep.

Must be close to five and I'm taking that meeting with the network tomorrow. Those Ivy League stiffs are gonna die for the concept. Sheer brilliance. *Nun Stalker.*

Nuns in a station wagon pick up some fruitcake hitchhiker on a desert and he terrorizes them for 48 hours. Solid gold. Gonna pull the heartland viewers like goddamned *Little House On The Prairie* with genitals. People love that crap. Pure entertainment. No different than what Shakespeare was doing. Stories. That's what we're talking here, folks. Stories. Not goddamned penicillin.

Screw that educational TV crap. Tribesmen getting culture. Kids with terminal diseases learning to love life again. Retarded people doing interpretive dances. Conversations with dolphins. Ballet.

Boooooooorrrrrrriiiinnnngggg! I'm in a friggin' coma, folks.

Now nuns in terror, with parched faces, genuflecting under the beating sun, talking penguin logic to some crazed rapist. That's friggin' television! That's friggin' drama! That's friggin' money in the bank. I goddamn love it! Gonna pull Nielsen families faster than that *Lesbian Cheerleaders* M.O.W. Jerry wrote last season. Another no talent sonofabitch. And cheap? Yeah, no shitsky, he's cheap. Wouldn't write a get-well card to his dying mother if he had to do it on spec. Total hack. Buy friggin' Bel Air off the residuals from every idea of mine he's ripped off.

Undercover Boy, I Dream of Mel. All my notions. And he stole every last one without flinching. *My* concepts!

They bring back the holocaust, Jerry goes first. The crooked slime. Send him to Hungaria with the ex. Get along great, exchanging favorite Chuck Manson stories. Friggin' vermin.

Belch... okay, off with the monogrammed robe and back into bed. Gotta get some... *holy Christ! What the hell is this?* A goddamned dummy in my bed! Who'd put a...? Hey, you know the answer to that one. Marty, Sam and Jerry. The friggin' Putzola brothers. Anything for a laugh.

Jesus... check out this goddamn thing... it's all dressed and made up to look like me. My hat's off to you, you putzes. You went all out. Unless... wait a minute. *Wait one friggin' minute.* This is too good a gag for those pinheads. Must be Mickey and Andy. Ever since they created *Future Waitress*, it's special effects coming out the wazoo, day and night, everywhere I go.

Rubber baked potatoes at Ma Maison. Spring-loaded snakes in my Ferrari's gas tank, graffiti on the yacht. Okay... jig's up, putzarooneys.

Alright, boys, get your goddamn dummy out of my bed! Got that meeting with the network tomorrow, gotta get some sleep.

No reaction.

Screw 'em. I'll move the bastard myself. (Groan) Je... *sus*... heavy sonof... Oh, *Christ!* Oh, *Jesus friggin' Christ!* Stand back, pal. Get away from the thing! It's *warm*. The friggin' dummy is *warm!* Hair feels real too. I think it's *alive*.

Gotta do something. Think, putz, think. Okay, okay, grab the gun out of the drawer... easy... easy... got it!

Okay, jerk! Outta the bed. Outta the bed, now! Come on... come on. *Move*, dammit! Wake up, man. *Wake up!* She-itt! The dummy who ain't a dummy ain't waking. Jesus Christ... and I've got that meeting with the network first thing tomorrow. I'm gonna look like hell.

Come on, man, wake up... Oh, for Christ sake, why me?... This isn't happening. Goddammit... *Wake up!* Okay, creep, you want to play? I'll friggin' play. And it's your can on a 14-karat platter, buddy. Okay, back to the kitchen and call the cops.

They'll be here in a hot sec too, if they recognize the name. Especially after I created *Robot Police Dog* last season. Got a 45 share every week in third runs! I mean come on! Third runs! And I got full rights to the merchandising. Those friggin' paw-thongs cleaned up. And cops *love* the show!

Okay, okay. Stop pulling the pudola, schmuck, and tiptoe out of the bedroom already! Don't wake the creep while you're at it. Could be nuttier than the guy in the desert with the parched nuns. Christ, keep that stuff to yourself, huh?

Belch... Not now, putz. Quiet! Quiet!

Okay, down the hall.

Thank God, there's the friggin' kitchen up ahead. And there's the phone! Now you're talking, Jack. Safety, here I come. One call to the Bel Air patrol and it's sleepy time for old...

What the friggin' hell? What gives here?! It's the same guy in the kitchen, next to the fridge, holding a bottle of my bubbly water. Bastard, how'd he get in here so fast? Quiet... what's he doing? Doing nothing, that's what he's doing. Standing there not moving a goddamned muscle; stiff as a soap actor. Jesus, schmuck, you got to get your tiffany hams out of here, fast!

Okay... I'm leaving. But I don't want to go past this sonofabitch. He'll probably come out of this friggin' zombie trance soon as I head for the kitchen door and gore me with an ice pick. Oh, God, I'm feeling like a parched nun already. Feel that sun beating down. Okay, okay, enough soap opera. Get back down the hall and do a quick dissolve, schmuck.

Ain't going to get killed *now*. Forty-seven and still taken for thirty-seven. Houses in Aspen, and Martha's Vineyard, plus the land in Maui, two yachts at Newport, half ownership in Topo's Italian restaurant and chicks coming from every which way. Redheads, brunettes, blondes, Peroxided negroes. They all want it *bad*. And I ain't about to disappoint them. No way, jack. I got everything going for me.

No goddamned zombie ying-yang is gonna munch *me* out of existence.

Okay, down the hall and let's get out of here. Alright, I'm practically to the door and out of this madhou... Oh, my God. *Oh, my God.*

He's at the hall table the ex gave me, reading the trades. How can he do it? How can he move so fas... Oh, Christ, he's still standing in the kitchen, holding the bubbly water from France. But he's also standing *here* reading the trades. There's two of the friggin' creepo monstrosities! And I'll bet that one in the bed is still in the bed. Okay... go ahead, look in the hall mirror...

You got it, boobie. There he is. Sleeping in the bed, all zombied out. Jesus Christ! Can't be happening. Too much Valium. I'm flipping out. I'm cracking. Listen to me, I'm whining. Whining!

Quiet fool, quiet!...Sorry, it's just this is scaring the mid-season replacements out of me! You know what's really crazy? And I'm talking bona fide electro-shock...*they all look like me!* That's the act three twist. All three of the goddamned zombies look exactly like me.

Ex-friggin'-zactly! I feel a pain in my chest.

What next? Dead nuns falling out of my closet? The garbage disposal weekend crazies grinding me into ninety-percent-tax-bracket caviar? Funny, putz, funny. Keep your thoughts to yourself, okay? Jesus, you gotta get your rich ass outta this place before more of them show and decide to throw a banquet with you as mogul du jour. Take the Rolls and get going! *Fuck!*

The keys. They're in the kitchen, hanging on the hook next to the fridge. You jerk! Hitchcock's gotta be around here somewhere. This is just too sick.

Forget the keys, schmuck. Listen to me; forget the Rolls, understand? Just get out of here and run down the road and scream for help. Someone will hear. You're famous. They'll know you from the talk shows. Mention Merv. Okay, back down the hall toward the front door...quietly, quietly...almost there. Heading for the front door. Grab that knob and get out of this joint. Okay turn the bastard.

I said *turn the bastard*. You're not listening...oh, yes I am. It's locked, goddammit!

Belch...

Great...locked. You forgot, Einstein: the whole friggin' place is on the security lock. You gotta get out. Think, putz...think. Alright, goddammit, there is a way. But you gotta go back into the bedroom and turn off the system.

Sure, why not? Probably gonna die anyway. Okay, back into the bedroom and get right next to that first zombie freak. Maybe strike up a chat. Ask about the family. Probably knows Sam. God,

I'm feeling like hell. Must be the friggin' flu or something. Whole body feels weak. Like I'm going to pass out. Relax, you're just delirious like that ballet dancer with gonorrhea you did for *Man From U.N.C.L.E.*

Better sit down on the sofa.

Zonk...here I am, sitting, scared out of my mind. Lovely visual schmuck. God, my head...so weak. Got to get over to the big velvet couch. Stretch out. Get off this piece of ritzy cah-cah the ex picked up in Florence. What do friggin' Italians know about couches, anyway? Leave them to their film festivals and pasta. Bunch of fags. Even the homosexuals. Ha! Now there's a joke for you. Even the homos, Jesus...

Okay, onto the big couch and lay down. Easy, easy. Lay down and close the eyes. God, I feel like I'm dying. Gotta get outta this horror house. Hey, how's that for a title, Sam? *Garbage Disposal Horror House.* Yeah, same to you, you monkey dick. God, I can feel my hand trembling. Look at it, it's tremb...Jesus...I must be losing my mind! Christ, the friggin' fingers are fading. Disappearing right off my arms! This ain't funny anymore.

Please, God, I never ask you for anything but to give Sam migraines...please, what's going on?

I'm getting scared. Look, putz, there's nothing wrong, okay? You had too much to drink, got to bed too late and you're flipping out. Maybe you got gas or something. It's just a friggin' nightmare. Friggin' sensitivity ganging up on you. Well, screw sensitivity. It never got anybody anywhere, right? So take a Valium and go to sleep, will you? Got that big meeting with the network tomorrow and you're gonna be Yoplait at this rate.

Alright, if you're not convinced, go ahead and open your eyes and check. Guarantee you the body's back intact. Ain't nobody in this mansion but you, your money and your friggin' paranoia. I'm telling you. Hands are back...so are the arms. No more Venus de Milo. Really, I swear.

Trust me.

Okay...eyes open...one-two-three and presto-friggin'-*chango*...

Oh, God...

Oh, God, he's still staring at me. Or me at him. Or me at me. Cute, cute. Always good with the words, eh, schmuck?

Lotta good it's doing you now. Your arms and legs are still gone. So what are you going to do? Get a job as a torso in one of Sam's sensitive cinematic epics? Jesus, I can see through my stomach. It's fading like a friggin' out-of-work star. The Incredible Shrinking Putz...

I've been friggin' poisoned. That's gotta be it. *Marty.*

Didn't give him a Rolls last year after he packaged that *Killer Hypoglycemics* feature with those podiatrists looking for a tax shelter. He *poisoned* me. It's gotta be him. Marty, I'm coming after you soon as I can get up. Friggin' murderer!

Oh, oh, the creep across from me's starting to twitch more. Jesus, what was that down the hall? It's that one reading the trades. He's coming this way! Dammit, stay where you are, creep!

God, I'm getting so weak. I can't think straight. I hear footsteps coming from the bedroom and the kitchen. Getting closer. Jesus, what the hell was that out of the corner of my eye?! Down the hall, schmuck...it was down the hall...it's that one reading the trades ...he's coming this way. *Closer!*

Why is this happening? All I ever wanted to do was direct. Marty, if you did this to me, you'll never work in this town aga...

Belch...not now, schmuck...

Friggin' Hollywood. Bunch of friggin' leeches. Gotta get out of this business and do something important. Oh, Christ, they're getting closer. They're right here. This is worse than friggin' reruns of *Gilligan's Island*.

Gotta get out of this friggin' town and go somewhere and do some thing import... Gotta friggin' start over somewhe... Gotta frig...

Bel...

The gurney was loaded and in seconds the ambulance wailed through the plush canyons of Bel Air, headed for UCLA Medical Center.

The two officers stood outside the huge mansion watching the ambulance disappear.

"Christ, he was the creator of *Robot Police Dog*," said the taller one.

"Love that show," said the shorter one. "Best damn thing on the air."

The two watched the Los Angeles sky twinkle through smog.

"Medics said heart attack," the taller one finally said.

The shorter one stared at the mansion, thoughtfully. "Know what's odd? Looking around that mansion there were some really weird things. I mean why would a guy have identical monogrammed robes lying on the floor in practically every room?"

The taller officer thought that one over, lit a Winston and shrugged.

"Who the hell knows," he said. "Maybe he had one for every room? Every mood? Money makes people eccentric, I mean... what the hell..." Cigarette smoke emptied from his mouth in a little cannon blast. "Hey, I was trying to remember... what did they call this guy? King of the Play-offs or some fuckin' thing?"

"No, no," his shorter partner corrected, "*Spin-offs*. King of the Spin-offs. Guy had more spin-offs on the air than anybody."

"Right, right," said the taller one and the two tiny men fell silent and stared up at the giant mansion as if expecting something.

Then, taking the cue, in every room of the mansion a T.V. set turned on. And on every single one, *Robot Police Dog* barked its opening credits, bit some bad guys, and went into a commercial.

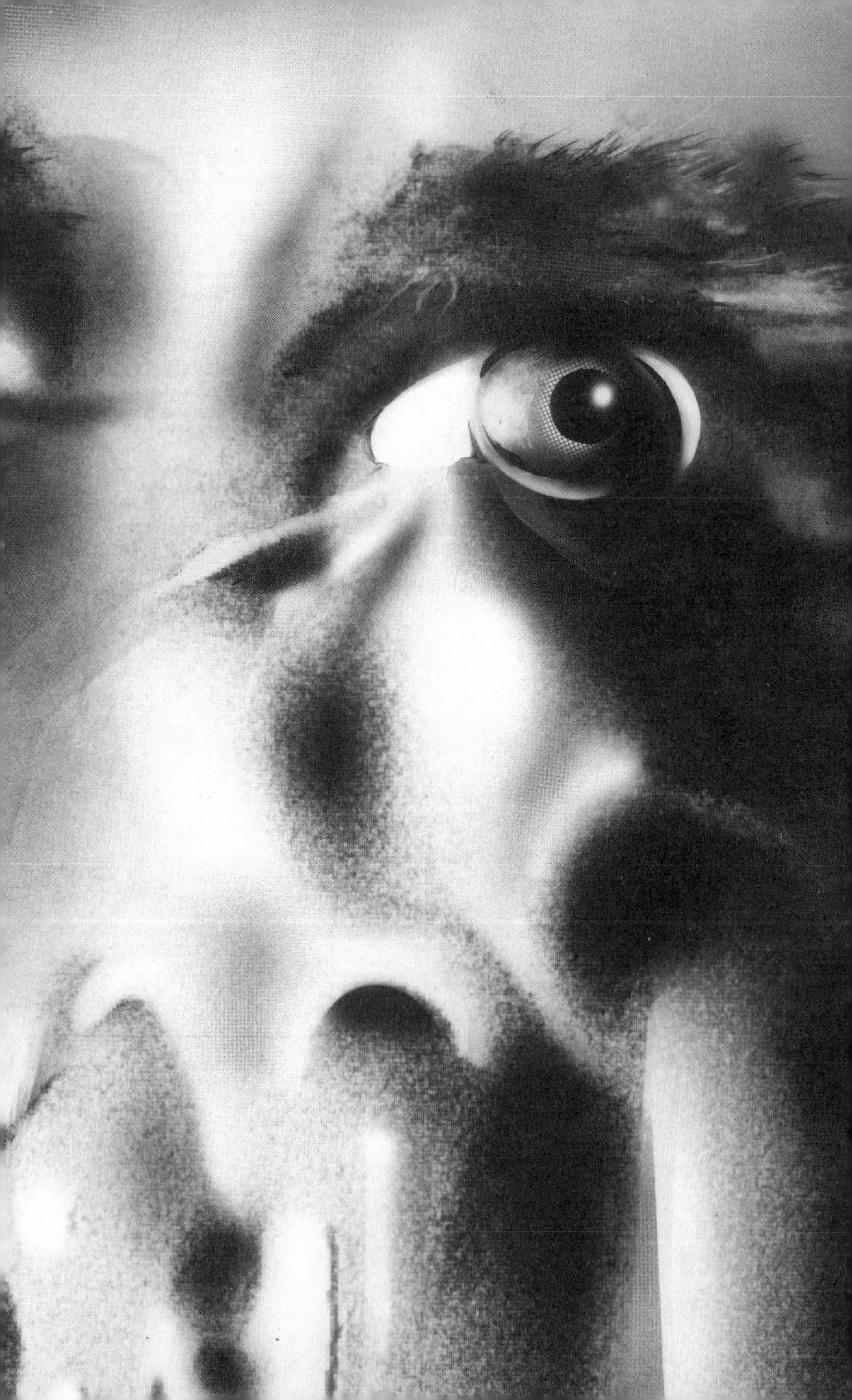

MUGGER

NOV. 1997
NEW YORK SHITTY (ha-ha)

Dear Sally,

WELL, luck's pickin' me up off my ugly face. Eddie and me got some hot ones tonight but I think we're on the outs even so. Check out what happened:

We're on 40th and Temple right? The Street was dark and smelled like death-puke, as usual and Eddie all-of-a-sudden sees this freako, right? So he sticks the thing in, yanks out the gooeys and the nutcase starts screamin'. We had the gooeys in our hands, pulsin' and jumpin'. So we snipped the slimeys that were holdin' 'em in and stuck the gooeys in our freezo-bag. Then we held down this screamin' nutcase and Eddie sewed his two holes up real snug, just weavin' the ol' needle through zip-zap, just like that. Real neat lookin'.

Then Eddie, he says to me, "hey man, we're fuckin' outta here." And he tells me to pour some alcohol all over this guy's face. So the guy tries to reach up to me from the dark ground and I just kick him away and pour the stuff on him and the nutcase just screams and Eddie yells at him and tells him to shut the fuck up.

So me and Eddie haul outta there and hit some old freakos a few more blocks up, right? Eddie gets their gooeys while I hold 'em down and after we sew 'em and sauce 'em, we go to the Creepo and he offers up practically nothin' for what we got in the pouch 'cuz the gooeys are too old. Have cat'rats, or some bullshit. Says half of it ain't any good after he tests it on the whizmos and gizmos and aren't we a couple dumb pricks for hittin' old freakos.

So, Eddie gets real hot and tells the guy we can unload it somewhere else and the Creepo just laughs and finally Eddie and me get in a big argument and I say let's take what he's offerin' and Eddie says, fuck what he's offerin'. So, Eddie grabs me and throws me against the Creepo's metal cage and some blood leaks out of my mouth and I get nutso and kick Eddie hard in the balls and he starts howlin' and I take the freezo-pouch and hand it over to the Creepo and take the cash and split.

Tell you one thing, Sally, me and Eddie run into each other, forget it man. Bet he's pissed. So now, I got me some dog dinner and I'm writin' to you to tell you how much I miss you and wanna marry you. I want you to hurry back home and not make me crazy. I'm gonna get you outta that place. We gotta be together. Hope they're not making you bloat-up all the time. It really pisses me off. This is bullshit.

Love,
Marky (your boyfriend)

Marky fell back on the trashed mattress and sighed, missing Sally and trying to think of ways to get her out of the population farm. It was going to be a motherfucker and he knew it.

He lit up some shit and fried his head. Looked up at the dripping pipes, remembering the first time.

It had been in the morning. He hadn't eaten in two weeks and some of the Creepos were paying cash for organs that weren't hurt too badly by the storm. So, he and Eddie, his oldest and best buddy, had run across a fucked-up bum, cut the guy open and ripped him off. Took what they could, sold it.

That night, they'd eaten like kings. Cans of every flavor they wanted: fish, chicken. Man, those were days. Like taking candy from babies. But now the whole world was paranoid. People didn't go out much. Or they wore fucking steel mesh. When you found them, you went for the gooeys. And you had to move fast—the competition was sicker than sick.

But that first time ... man. Candy from a baby.

Marky smiled to himself and tried to sleep but he kept thinking of screaming faces and terrified expressions and dripping, red holes where eyes used to be. It passed soon enough and as sky-vehicles roamed outside the burned-out skyscraper, firing search beams, he rolled over and fell asleep.

THE DARK ONES

THE PAIN hadn't stopped for hours.

It seared his shoulder, and moving was making it worse.

He shuddered, barely able to go on.

Only an hour ago.

The family had been together, the children playing in their favorite hiding place. Beautiful children, children of their own. The two of them had watched so proudly. They were lucky. Children were rare these days. And after her first terror with the Dark Ones, having a family had seemed impossible.

It was getting bad again.

What did they use that made their spears hurt so much? He'd felt it splay the skin out when it buried itself in his back. It was like no pain he'd ever felt.

She and the children had escaped. He wasn't sure where. North, perhaps. Away from where the Dark Ones could try and murder them.

He knew the children must be tired, wherever they were. To be chased by the Dark Ones would be a nightmare for them.

He, too, was tired. But he had to keep moving.

Night.

His eyes ached. He couldn't see far ahead.

The Dark Ones might turn back. He knew they were frightened of the blackness. It could be his chance.

He stopped to breathe for a moment, and the cooling air soothed inside.

But seconds later, he screamed.

The Dark Ones had shot again. The thing was twisting in his neck, and he shrieked for it to stop. He felt as if he were going to lose consciousness as it tore and burned inside.

She and the children.

He had to keep moving and see them once more. He loved them so. He had to get to them before the Dark Ones found him. *Keep moving*, he told himself.

Keep moving.

But the pain was spreading.

He looked back and saw the Dark Ones coming closer, shouting with glee. He couldn't breathe. *I'm growing weaker*, he realized. *Slowing down.*

He began to cry. He didn't want to die without seeing her and the children one last time. But the pain was getting worse.

He pleaded for someone to help.

Then, suddenly, he felt it: a rupturing explosion in his shoulder, and everything went black.

A thin rain fell as the laughing voices neared and circled slowly, looking at what they had done.

The body had been ripped and shredded and oily blood splashed everywhere, dyeing everything it touched.

As they worked, joking among themselves, they didn't notice her watching.

With the children there beside her, she saw them haul her mate upward, and began to weep. Then, moaning a cry of eternal loss which rang to the depths, she and the children plunged their great bodies back into the bloody sea.

As they fled, seeking the safety of the deeper waters, the echoes of their cries were answered by the haunted, far away responses of the few who remained.

HOLIDAY

IT WAS SUNSET. The inn was settling into night and vacationers wandered up from the beach, tired and sunburned. It was very hot in Bermuda—like a desert with an azure sea seeping from one side.

The waiter brought my drink and I rested my feet on the patio wall overlooking the ocean. As the sea churned easily, wearily from its day, a man sat down next to me. His hair was white and there wasn't much of it. His skin was fair, almost pink, cheeks sunburned and high. About sixty to seventy, I figured.

"Mind?" he asked, half-finished drink in hand.

"I could use the company." He seemed harmless enough.

He settled down into the chaise, and together we watched the waves spreading over the sand and retreating. Birds with long, thin, legs sprinted awkwardly over the sand and eventually lifted skyward.

"Flyin's a hell of a thing," he observed, after a long sip.

"I can't do it," I agreed, and he smiled.

"Where you from?" he asked, eyes sizing me.

"Los Angeles. Just down for some sun and free time." A waiter in penguin-proper sidled over and the man ordered us another round.

"My treat," he offered. "Makes me feel good."

I nodded thanks as he winked paternally.

"What's your name?" he asked, taking another swallow.

"Karl," I answered, ready for trouble. The way I saw it, paternal winkers always made trouble for you one way or another.

"Pretty nice," he appraised its sound, "Karl...yeah, pretty damn nice."

"Thanks," I said, growing less than fascinated with the exchange. I decided not to ask his name. Why wave the red cape.

"Say, Karl, do you mind if I ask you a personal question?"

No objection, so he went ahead.

"What did you get for Christmas last year?"

I swallowed a mouthful of ice after crushing it to bits.

"What?" I was starting to feel the liquor.

"For Christmas...what did you get?"

"You serious?" He was looking a bit sloshy himself, wiping his mouth with one hand, thoughtfully, drunkenly.

He gestured away my stinginess and I nodded unenthusiastically.

"Power saw from the wife, shirts and a record from the kids, binoculars from the folks, and a wine-making kit from the people in my department." I tinkled the ice around in my glass. "Oh, and this magazine I subscribe to, *Realtors Life*, sent me a barometer with an escrow chart. Helps you figure percentages."

The other round arrived and he paid the waiter. Tipped him good.

He sighed as he mumbled through my recitation of gifts. "What was the record?" he asked.

"Music from *Hatari*. Horrible stuff. Oboes imitating rhinos, you know?"

He nodded and swallowed half his new drink with a liquidy gobble. We didn't say anything else for a few minutes. Some of the inn workers came by, and lit the tiki torches and we watched them. Bugs were flying around, drawn to the glow. We swatted one or two.

"I love it down here," he said, voice blurry. "Just wish the hell I had the time to get away more often."

He looked at me with bloodshot eyes. "But in distribution... who has time to vacation?"

How the hell did I know? I sold condos and houses and made deals for closing costs and termite inspections. Dullest stuff in the world. Distribution was for pamphlets dropped from helicopters, as far as I could tell.

"Yeah," I answered, being polite. Why get a paternal winker mad if it could be avoided?

The sea was glowing from a butter-colored moon, and the man shifted in the chaise.

"How'd you like the power saw?" he asked.

"Not bad. Blades were pot metal, though. Break like icicles." Nosy guy.

"Yeah, I know the one." He reached a hand out to mine. We were both woozy. "I like you," he said. Drunks always said that, in my experience.

"I like you, too," I said. "But I didn't catch the name." When they stick their hands out, you have to ask.

He winked at me as our hands met, under that butter-moon.

"Santa," he whispered, leaning in close, breath like a scythe.

I looked at him with a half-smile.

"Beg your pardon?"

"Santa," he repeated, nodding happily.

"As in Claus?"

"Well, of course. What else?"

I tried to not look any different. Why upset him?

"Sorry," I said.

He pulled back and yawned.

"Yeah, well... anyhow, I'll be leaving first thing in the morning. Have to get back to my place up north. Me and the wife have tons of work." He laughed a little; a tiny, drunken, aren't-things-ironic laugh. "Christ, it's already bloody May. Practically no time to do anything. Glad we had a chance to shoot the breeze, though."

He stretched and yawned again, spilling some of his drink onto the patio where just he and I sat, the warm breezes blowing.

"Oh," I said, watching him from the corner of my eye. *The insane look different*, my father once told me. *Just look closely and you can see it*.

"Anyhow, you have a nice trip back to..."

"Los Angeles," I reminded him, finishing off my drink.

"Right," he nodded. "Say, care for another drink? I can have the waiter get you another...just say the word."

I declined the offer. Don't get indebted to nuts. Another piece of advice. That one from my mother.

He turned to go.

"Hey, by the way, Karl..."

Yes, Santa? I couldn't bring the words to my mouth.

"Yes?" I said.

"Sorry about all that junk you got. I just can't seem to get those little bastards of mine to turn out any decent work. But I'll try and drop off something this year you'll like."

I must have smirked.

"Need an address?" I asked. I was smirking for sure.

He stopped dead in his tracks, looking hurt.

"Address? You putting me on?" His eyes were still twinkling, but they looked a little miffed. "I'm Santa Claus. I know where you live."

He stared at me and I stared back. Hard to know what to say at a moment like that.

"Tell me something," I said, "how come when I was eight, you didn't bring me that autographed picture of Joe DiMaggio I asked for? I wrote to you and everything."

He looked uncomfortable. "Well, sometimes it doesn't go the way I'd like," he managed, looking away in what seemed like troubled thought.

"Oh," I said, "sorry. Didn't mean to put you on the spot."

He nodded, seeming to accept the apology, though obviously put off. I suddenly felt awful.

"Forget it," he said quietly. "It's not your fault. I probably shouldn't be so candid about things."

His voice sounded vulnerable and a little sad.

"The wife keeps telling me to keep my big mouth closed. People just don't like to hear about what I do for a living." He shrugged. "Scares them or something...I don't completely understand it myself."

I looked into his moist, open eyes.

"How come no beard?" I asked.

He rubbed at his cheeks with a rough hand.

"Shave it off when I come down here. Only way to get any decent sun. But I get a burn every damn time."

As I watched him from the corner of my eye, he sighed and grabbed at his fat stomach, tucking his shirt in. "Gotta lose some weight...you don't know any good diets do you? But no fad things...something that'll work."

I shook my head no, feeling kind of sorry for him. Nuts, but sweet, I figured.

"Hey, sure you don't want to stay for another round?" I asked. No harm in *my* asking, I thought.

He smiled, glad we were getting along again.

"Nah...I should get back and get some sleep. Leaving in the morning, Karl."

I stood up to see him off.

"Well, nice meeting you, Santa."

That time it felt good.

"Same here, Karl," he said. "And like I said before, don't worry about this year." He winked at me, "I'll see to it you get something really nice; something you'll like."

I looked at him and smiled. "Thanks."

"Don't stay out too late, Karl," he said, and in a couple of seconds he was gone, tottering back to his room.

Well, I sat out there until midnight and thought a lot about Santa. His twinkling eyes and his fat stomach and his thin silver hair.

He sure did look like Santa Claus.

But, I mean really, truthfully, honestly, what was I supposed to think?

The man was clearly on a permanent holiday upstairs. No dial tone.

So, for another twenty minutes or so I watched the black Caribbean hissing over coral and finished off another drink.

Somehow, I finally made it back to my bungalow and thought for a little while in the dark. Sure, Santa Claus had looked like Santa Claus. But if looks were all it took, a lot of people could be a lot of people they weren't. The world would be crazy. Out of control.

And thinking sleepy thoughts along that line, I fell deeper into my pillow and nodded off.

The following morning, as I checked out, I peered at the desk clerk, going about his prissy duties. I lifted my voice slightly as I observed him tabulating my bill.

"I was chatting with a gentleman last night. A Mr. Claus." Why explain the whole thing? Only be setting myself up, I figured.

But in a surprise turn, the clerk lit up, his mouth turning into a silly-looking O.

"Oh," he cooed, "I'm so glad you reminded me, sir. Mr. Claus left this morning..." He turned and grabbed something from the mail slots as he continued chattering. "Flying north I believe he said."

Now there's a surprise, I thought.

Then he handed me something as he spun back, smiling all the while.

A manila envelope.

And so the plot thickened, I thought. I thanked him, paid the bill, and found myself a fat couch to sink into.

A few feet away, a wedding cake fountain dribbled as I unsealed the envelope. Maybe an apology, I thought. Although a wanted poster would have been more appropriate.

But as I slid what was inside all the way out, my heart smoked to a stop.

It was a picture of smiling Joe with a fat-ended slugger raised over one confident shoulder. And it was made out to me.

Clipped to it was a handwritten note:

Dear Karl,

Was up late last night and couldn't sleep. Really sorry about that Christmas. '39 was a bad year for me. The war was starting up, and my helpers' hearts just weren't in their work. The world wasn't in very good shape then, Karl, and I had my hands full. Hope this makes up for it. Have a Merry Christmas.

Your drinking pal, Santa

P.S. Maybe I'll see you around the 25th.

I'll be looking for you, I thought, as I read the note, trembling like some delighted kid.

I'll be looking for you.

VAMPIRE

Man.
Late. Rain.
Road.
Man.
Searching. Starved. Sick.
Driving.
Radio. News. Scanners. Police. Broadcast.
Accident. Town.
Near.
Speeding. Puddles.
Aching.
Minutes.
Arrive. Park. Watch.
Bodies. Blood. Crowd. Sirens.
Wait.
Hour. Sit. Pain. Cigarette. Thermos. Coffee.
Sweat. Nausea.
Streetlights. Eyes. Stretchers. Sheets.
Flesh.
Death.
Shaking. Chills.

Clock. Wait.
More. Wait.
Car. Stink. Cigarette.
Ambulance. Crying. Towtruck. Bodies. Taken.
Crowd. Police. Photographers. Drunks. Leave.
Gone.
Street. Quiet.
Rain. Dark. Humid.
Alone.
Door. Out. Stand. Walk. Pain. Stare. Closer.
Buildings. Silent. Street. Dead.
Blood. Chalk. Outlines. Closer.
Step. Inside. Outlines. Middle.
Inhale. Eyes. Closed.
Think. Inhale. Concentrate. Feel. Breathe.
Flow.
Death. Collision. Woman. Screaming. Windshield. Expression.
Moment. Death.
Energy. Concentrate. Images. Exploding.
Moment.
Woman. Car. Truck. Explosion.
Impact. Moment.
Rush.
Feeling. Feeding.
Metal. Burning. Screams. Blood. Death.
Moment. Collision. Images. Faster.
Strength. Medicine. Trance.
Stronger.
Concentrate. Better.
Images. Collision. Stronger. Seeing. Death.
Moment. Healing. Moment.
Addiction.
Drug. Rush. Body. Warmer.
Death. Concentrating. Healing. Addiction. Drug.
Warmth. Calm.
Death. Medicine.

Death.
Life.
Medicine.
Addiction. Strong.
Leave.
Car. Engine. Drive. Rain. Streets. Freeway. Map.
Drive. Relax. Safe. Warm. Rush. Good.
Radio. Cigarette. Breeze.
Night.
Searching. Accidents. Death.
Life.
Dash. Clock. Waiting.
Soon.

INTRUDER

AT SIX-FIFTEEN, Relling broke in.

He glanced around the front hall nervously. He had to work fast; cash, jewelry, portable telequipment, something. His arm was hungry and he ached. Everybody he knew did. Lately it seemed like the whole world needed the shit. You did what you had to. Pain had him half in its mouth and he groaned. Too many fucking hours. He had to hurry. The beam of his glovelight scanned the dimness.

Then, from behind, a deep male voice froze him. It said, "You're intruding," and he whirled, dropping the crowbar.

The man was seven feet tall and dressed in black. Scooped cheeks, dead eyes. A fast-charge Air-Mailer was strapped to his right leg; .55, bore eleven with a hot point. Bad enough to burn a tunnel in the wall and melt three blocks if it was up high. The huge man stared without blinking and Relling felt his nerves twisting.

"Hey, sorry I fucked up, Mister. Wrong house, that's all." Relling backed toward the splinter-edged front door, clothes sticky with sweat, a runny smile puddling on his face. "No big thing, you know? Just got the wrong place... that's all. Okay?" His fingers searched for the door knob and he lifted a scared grin, staring at the humming cannon hanging on the man's leg. As he frantically grabbed the knob, the door deadbolted itself with an electric

CLICK and voltage knocked Relling to the entryway floor. He shook his head, stunned and the huge man looked down at him.

"No mistake," the man said with his deep voice.

Relling felt his guts tangle. There was something wrong with the man. As though he—

"Hey, come on, man…let me outta here, will ya?" Relling's eyes were crazed and he could feel his veins starved for the crank. Everything was hurting. The man stared at him without emotion.

"It was a fucking mistake, man! I'll pay for the damage!" He began to slam the door with the side of a fist. "Just let me out, I'll get the money!"

The huge man stared at him and Relling suddenly reached into a torn coat and offered his own gun, throwing it down, nodding; eager to make a deal. "Okay? It's worth what the door's gonna cost."

The huge man's gaze never wavered as he reached down to unholster the Air-Mailer. Relling lunged for the staircase and pounded up the steps, glancing back. The huge man had drawn his weapon and was thumbing down the pulse switch for close range. Relling dived to the landing floor just before he heard the *phloosh* and saw the laser bruise the walls blue. He whimpered as he scrabbled up and raced along the second story hallway, hearing the huge man's thudding footsteps on the staircase.

The hallway was dark and silent. Three doors, a narrow table pushed against the wall. A small window at the end of the hall emitted faint illumination from a roof-eave security spot. By its light, Relling moved frantically, grabbing door knobs and getting shocked, fingers curling from the current. The footsteps sounded louder, closer, and Relling crouched under the hall table, terrified, breathing hard. What the hell was wrong with the man? He'd offered to pay for the damage, offered his gun. The guy was fried-out. Blood-hungry. What did the goddamn freak *want?*

He saw the shadow of the huge man slowly coming down the hall like a dinosaur hunting for little men with spears to eat and crouched lower, body shaking. He watched the man's great boots step closer. Then past. He could see pants rustle, the shadow of the cannon held tightly; ready to Mail him. The man stopped at the end of the hall and opened the door there without receiving a shock. He looked inside the room. Relling licked his lips. If he could make it to the stairs, get down, retrieve his gun and blow away the front door lock. He tensed, ready to bolt.

But the huge man turned from the open doorway, walked back to the table and stopped. He kneeled to Relling's level and looked right at him. White teeth showed.

"Can't hide," said the man, raising the Air-Mailer.

Relling reared-up, throwing off the table. The huge man had the hallway blocked and Relling ran toward the window, grabbing its handle and yanking upward. An electric shock sawed at his arm muscles and he screamed. He looked back to see the huge man coming closer, lips drawn up in a torturer's grin.

Relling began to slam balled fists against the window and his hands were sliced wide by the breaking panes. With fast glances, he saw the huge man almost to him; staring, stalking. In panic, Relling kicked at the glass and shoved a leg through, clutching at the window handle, numb to the jolts of electricity spraying his insides.

The huge man raised the Air-Mailer as Relling finally made it partway through the window, thrashing wildly.

A laser *phloosh* filled the hall and the blue arc bathed everything as Relling screamed, blown through the window, silently falling to the lawn below.

Forty minutes later, the splintered front door opened and the owner came in, dropping his briefcase. He saw something from the corner of his eye and turned to see the huge man staring at him, Air-Mailer holstered. The huge man said nothing. The owner asked what happened.

"There was an intruder," said the huge man in an informing monotone. "Six-fifteen. Tool of entry—crowbar."

"Did you subdue him?"

The huge man made no expression. "I removed him. He had a weapon. He resisted. Total removal time, three minutes, eleven seconds."

The owner sighed irritably and crossed the entryway, walking straight toward the huge man and then through him, as if he weren't there. He stood before the wall-mounted control panel, face illuminated by the blinking light of the *Holographic Stalk System 6000.* He entered his secret code and in under one second the huge man instantly disappeared.

The owner went to the kitchen drawer and grabbed the system's manual, skimming it while calling the police to collect the body. He didn't understand why the system hadn't stunned and subdued the prowler as programmed and cradled the phone to his ear as his call was answered.

At four a.m. as the owner slept deeply, the wall-mounted control panel downstairs began to pulse. Somewhere in the wrongly installed circuits, the *Stalk System* was replaying the earlier chase and removal of the prowler. In several seconds, the memory storage re-played it thousands of times and the circuits pulsed faster.

The STUN-SUBDUE function brought no stimulation and the system silently re-programmed itself to only REMOVE from now on. It began to scan the house with a sensor beam for intruders and finally located one. As the circuits pulsed wildly, the huge man dressed in black materialized in the entryway and began to head upstairs to the owner's bedroom.

It was removal time.

DUST

TWO MINUTES since he'd blinked.

He clutched his coffee frozenly. Sweat trickled. His eyes followed as the dust drifted onto the booth table, warm and slow. He grabbed a menu and propped it against the window, blocking the klieg of sun. Quickly scanned the coffee shop for angry eyes. Eyes that didn't understand. Stupid eyes shifting in blank, doomed faces.

He lifted the bleached mug, sipped coffee and suddenly tasted a crawling tickle on his tongue.

It was in there.

He spit the black liquid onto the table top and watched the dust floating. Swimming.

Multiplying.

There was no way to stop it. He'd tried; every day he'd tried. Even harder at night. Trying desperately to sleep when the sun had gone down and the dust hid in darkness.

He would lock his apartment tight, doors and windows sealed, and go to work to capture the marauding downpour. Standing in a corner of the room, not moving, flashlight gripped. He would listen and wait for minutes. Once for hours; not wanting the dust to sense his presence.

When he finally heard it in front of him, its horrid tinkle like far away sleighbells, he would shock the dust by thumbing on the flashlight and blinding it. Then, he would start the vacuum cleaner, and stare in hunter's fixation as the dust screamed, sucked into a long nozzle he held in his hand.

Smiling at the agonized shrieks, he would move slowly through the apartment, passing the nozzle back and forth, its fat throat swallowing the helpless dust until the slaughter was total; the room safe for sleep.

But he didn't sleep well. He knew the dust would be back by morning, sneaking in through cracks and vents as he twisted with nightmares.

It couldn't be stopped. It was falling everywhere, twenty-four hours a day; an endless supply of smothering, swirling horror. No matter where he went to escape it, to fool it and hide, it would always be there, drifting to the ground like invading parachutists; fearless, secret.

He watched the sunbeam that had moved to the side of the menu. Its yellow straightness was a perfect landing strip for the dust which floated closer to the ground, making noises he'd come to hate. The amusement of the dust; laughing, ridiculing. The arrogant sounds it made as it fell closer, ready to land, ready to join the billions of others. The plans it had; he heard those, too. He'd heard them from the start, when there had been only advance parties descending from the sky. Nobody else seemed to question it. But he'd always known more would come and that time only made it worse, offering the perfect means to chart the inevitable suffocation.

He left the table, positioned goggles, placed a handkerchief over his mouth and walked out onto the city street past a store window. He glanced up. Dust coated the window and its weightless eyes watched him. He hurried on and approached a pedestrian crossing where he waited. He looked down to see dust on the tips of his shoes and bent quickly to wipe it off with the handkerchief, feeling the dust's sticky voltage on the cotton. He threw the white square onto the sidewalk, then lit it on fire with matches from his pocket. As flames rose, he moved closer to hear the dust burning to death.

That night, he decided to fight the dust using different

methods, knowing it must be deceived so it couldn't predict his strategy; his advantage. At just past eleven, he rose in darkness. He had been waiting, feigning sleep, listening since sundown to the dust's hidden murmurings. It was secreted in the weave of the curtain fabric, and he heard it scheming, watching for his unguarded sleep. He moved in silence to the tattered curtains, a thick board raised over his shoulder. The sound of the board striking the drab material over and over was mixed with the panicked screams of the dust as it grabbed at one another, forming stunned clumps which clouded helplessly.

When he'd forced it all out, he grabbed his vacuum and started it, holding the nozzle in sweaty hands, sweeping it through the air. The sounds of tiny death filled the apartment, screaming and crying until nothing could be heard. He figured several hundred thousand had died. Finally, he slept, relaxed snores drawing him through what little night remained.

By morning, the city stared at a murky sun which had turned almost brown and he rose to fight the dust. He pulled open his curtains and drained white at what he saw. Moving in, from the west, was a mile-wide wall of dust, a bronze wave that curled closer.

He dressed in silence, knowing what he must do. The air-tight jumpsuit was zipped, heavy boots pulled on. The portable battery-pack vacuum was harnessed to his back. Goggles positioned. He pulled on gloves, clutched the vacuum nozzle, went downstairs and kicked open the front door.

As he walked through the silent city which had been dead for half a century, his mind flooded with images of his children and wife. Friends, and parents. Dogs. Christmas. Laughter. The viral clouds which swept the Mars settlement had destroyed them; taken everything. Fighting the dust was the only thing that kept him sane.

He turned on his portable vacuum and walked slowly toward the brown storm, which howled closer, killing everything it touched.

He had survived. He would survive.

He would win.

GOOSEBUMPS

...and so it was on that foul, moonlit eve, the fetid creature disappeared as inexplicably as it had spawned. And though Mr. Edworthy would never tell the good peoples of Frankshire what manner of obscene anguish he'd suffered, he would never forget.

For in that forgotten hamlet, on the farthest reaches of the Scottish coast, evil had entered not only the body of a man, but his very soul. Evil, which was finally, thank God, gone.

Or at least Mr. Edworthy thought it was.

Until suddenly, he felt that horrid, famished gnawing. The one he'd come to dread.

And the frightened townsfolk could hear his tortured screams as they lit torches and trod up the dirt road to Edworthy's farm.

But what they found was never spoken about again.

Nightmares were just as soon forgotten.

ANDY CLOSED the anthology and shivered.

Not a bad little horror story.

Not bad at all.

Nightfall was a terrific collection with a truly unnerving host of stories, including some of the finest horror he'd ever read. The one about the confessional haunted by the long dead priest had really shaken him. And the one about the circus fat man who ate his curious victims was an appalling fascination. But it was this last one, "Edworthy's Fate", which was beginning to really chill him.

As he slid under the covers, he placed the collection on the nightside table and turned off the light.

Bundling up, he shivered.

Christ, he had honest-to-God goosebumps covering his body.

These horror writers were *amazing*.

They knew precisely what it took to make your skin crawl. And once they had you hooked, their phrases and adjectives were like acids that ate away at your mind. When one of these stories worked, it virtually jumped off the page.

Andy noticed his stomach was on edge and smiled.

What better accolade to the writer of "Edworthy's Fate". Some hapless reader, lying in the dark, wide awake, stomach sashed by nerves.

Strange way to make a living, he thought.

Taking a breath, he tried to empty his mind of the loathsome images created by the story. As he did, he reached down to scratch the back of his left hand and felt something.

Damned mosquitos, he groaned, scratching the bitelike rise directly above his knuckles. Must have gotten in through the bathroom window. He was about to get up and close the window, but as he scratched harder, his eyes suddenly widened.

It was *moving*.

Under his skin, it had crept upward, toward the wrist, like an eye sliding from the bottom of its socket to the top.

He quickly turned on the light and his stomach twisted as he watched the tiny rise moving up his wrist. As it went, it pushed the skin outward, making his forearm swell slightly, as if a stray air bubble were lost in his system.

As it travelled further up Andy's arm, the rise left a red trail, causing his arm hair to stand out.

For a moment, too frightened to move, he finally reached for the phone and began to dial his doctor's exchange. But he was stopped by the sensation of the bump racing up his left arm and bolting across his shoulders before hurtling down his right arm into his hand.

Shocked, Andy dropped the receiver and lurched into his dressing area to look in the full length mirror.

He slowly raised his right arm and his mouth went dry. There in the center of his palm was the bump, pulsing slightly; stirring like a trapped animal.

In dead silence, he watched the thing continue to swim about beneath the skin on his palm, coursing from side to side in random patterns.

As if it were waiting impatiently for something.

But for what, he wondered, deciding to try and feel it. He could see how far it was stretching his skin but wasn't sure how large it actually was.

Feeling as though he were losing his mind, he cautiously arced his left hand over and allowed it to hover over the right palm. Taking a deep breath, he lunged down on the bump, trying to grab it with his left hand.

But it had already moved and he watched in panic as the bump began to move up his right arm. As it did, it left an inch-wide track of red, swollen skin in its wake.

Sickened, Andy grabbed at it again as it climbed above his elbow. But it had moved too quickly for him and was now sliding to his shoulder. Hysterically, he slapped at his shoulder, trying to stop the bump from moving any further. But though he could feel the lump of it beneath his hand, it quickly slipped away and began to move across his chest.

And as it did, something new began to happen.

As Andy darted back into his bedroom, thrashing from his pajama top, he felt a squeezing, gnawing agony beginning to cover the tingling areas where the bump had been.

Looking in his bureau mirror, he could see ropy bruises where the strands of inflamed tissue had been. And as the bump crossed over his chest, a torturous burning filled his torso.

The thing seemed to be sawing through his flesh.

He knew there was no way he could drive himself to the emergency hospital. The thing would somehow try to stop him and he shuddered at the thought of what it would do if he tried.

Suddenly, the scalding pain had returned, and the bump raced more savagely through his body.

Gasping, he ran into the kitchen and yanked open a drawer. But as he did, the bump slid around his naked waist like a cinch. In seconds it travelled to his back and settled on the spine where it began to torture anew.

As it moved further up his spine, he could feel it squeezing and tearing at the spongy tissue, trying to get at the nerve braids.

Screaming in pain, Andy threw himself onto the floor and lay on his back, pressing hard, trying to crush the bump. As he did, he could feel it boring further into his spinal sheath, devouring nerves. As the bump continued to gorge through his body, feasting on the pulpy nerve junctions and carving through the skin, just a quarter of an inch under the surface, Andy's face turned bright red.

He was screaming but no sound came.

Sprawled fitfully on the kitchen floor, he looked down to see the bump slowly making its way up his leg toward his internal organs.

His mouth opened in revulsion as the bump stopped for a moment, directly above his appendix and intestines and began to pulse, again.

For the first time, he could see it was getting bigger, as it ingested his living flesh for nourishment.

Andy felt like vomiting.

The bump began to gnaw at his intestines and his screams of dread returned.

For the first time, he now knew what the thing needed to survive.

As it continued to feast upon him, Andy struggled to stand, stumbling for the kitchen drawer; reaching into it.

From its interior, he withdrew a huge butcher knife which glistened under the fluorescent lighting.

But in seconds, as if it had seen, the bump moved.

And this time Andy cried out, clutching his hands to his face and shrieking.

Somehow, the bump had moved to his face and was now causing his features to distort as it made its way under the skin, devouring what it could.

Holding the knife firmly, Andy staggered into the bedroom bathroom and watched himself in the mirror.

On the right cheek was the bump.

Only now it was much bigger; the size of an egg. And as Andy watched spellbound, the bump rotated beneath the surface of the bruised skin, showing something on its opposite side.

The incisors were vague under the quilt of his skin, but there was no doubt they were starting to move.

And as they did, he felt the pain, immediately.

The bump was beginning to consume.

Andy could actually hear the sound of his facial meat being ravaged as the insatiable bump continued to grow with each tearing piece it ate.

And though his screams caused him to tremble, he didn't hesitate.

He held the knife directly at his face, and began stabbing at the monstrosity.

As he did, it averted his slashing lunges, as if anticipating every move.

His face bled profusely from deep gashes, and Andy stared through the wash of red covering his eyes to see where the bump would show next.

He screamed for it to go away, blood spraying from his lips.

But as he howled for it to leave, he suddenly felt something in his mouth, filling it like an inflating bladder.

And though he tried to scream, the bump muffled everything, attaching itself to his tongue.

Andy put the knife to his mouth and opened wide. Peering at himself in the mirror, he began to thrust the knife into his mouth, convulsively, stabbing at the bump and causing it to squirt fluid from itself.

It tasted acrid and sloshed down Andy's throat as he continued to stab.

Then it happened.

Suddenly, the bump was gone and Andy could now see only the raw mutilation of his mouth, dripping its bloody wetness down his shirt.

Searching his body, he couldn't see or feel the bump *anywhere*.

For a moment, all pain stopped.

Inexplicably, the thing had ceased and all was calm.

Or at least Andy thought it was.

Until suddenly pain began in his forehead. Then, horribly, his brow began to inflate outwardly, causing him to resemble some terror-stricken primitive. The brow continued to jut out further and the wrenching pain thickened all around, pile-driving through his skull.

Then, in a blinding insight, he knew what must be happening, as he felt his shrieking brain finally being descended upon.

And though the neighbors could hear his screams echoing over the streets, no one called the police until it was far too late.

It was a warm afternoon and the countryside lolled comfortably under a summer sky. As he snipped lovingly at the carnations, the bell caught his attention.

Yawning, he strolled over toward the mailman's bicycle. The mailman strummed the tiny bell, which was attached to his handlebars, one last time, and smiled.

"Lots for you today, Mr. McCauley."

The old man smiled easily. As he stepped closer, he drew a deep breath, taking in the beautiful flowers which bloomed in abundance before his quaint country home. Insects buzzed around the colorful garden.

"Bills, no doubt," chuckled the old man, accepting the handful of envelopes.

"Think there's one in there from your agent in the states, sir."

The old man's eyebrows lifted with interest, and he sifted through the envelopes. In seconds he'd opened it.

As he read the letter, the mailman looked at him inquisitively. "Sell that horror novel, did you?"

The old man shook his head, with a relaxed sigh.

"No, those publishers in New York haven't made their final offer yet."

The mailman made a look of disappointment.

The old man peered up at him with a glint.

"There is a bit of good news, though. You know that story of mine you hate so much? It's been requested as a reprint in another anthology."

"How many times is that, now?"

"Over two hundred," answered the man, about to turn and putter up the path to his house.

" 'Edworthy's Fate' just never gave me goosebumps," said the mailman.

"Lucky you," smiled the old man, heading back to his flowers, humming a gentle little song.

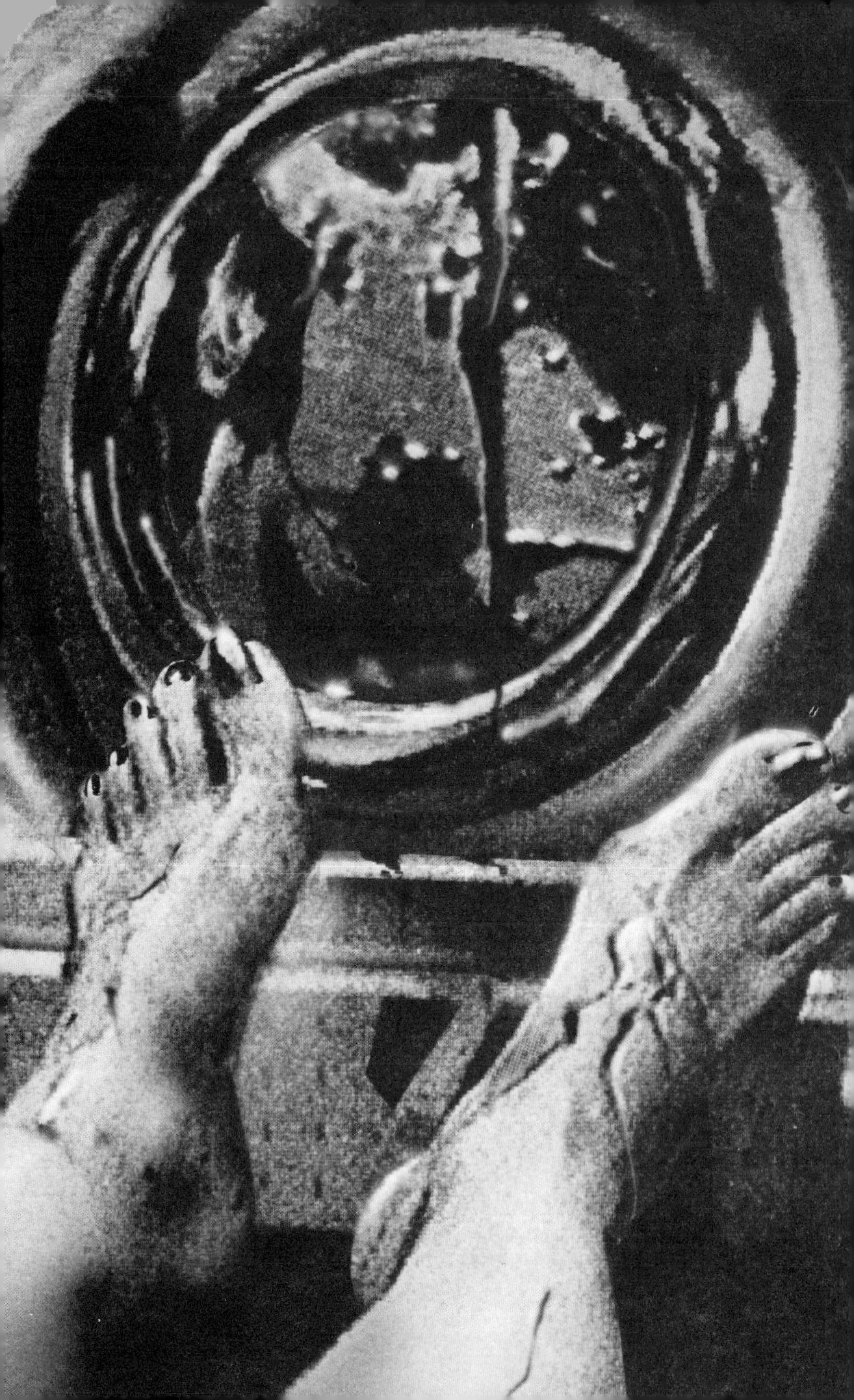

MOBIUS

HEAT BLISTERING. Head leaned, grinning at the sun. About forty. Swollen, staring eyes. The man in the tie stared at him. Spoke calmly. Smoked.

"Ready to talk?"

"I want some Coke or somethin'... I'm thirsty."

"Later."

"I'm thirsty."

Words thick. Hard to understand. Lips rising, falling, chalk dry.

"Let's answer some questions first. How many people have you killed?"

"Isn't there nothin' around here to drink?"

"Seventy-three, that's alot, Jimmy. You're a vicious man."

"That how many?"

"You don't remember killing them?"

"Hey, man... I'm fucking *thirsty*."

"Ever been to L.A.?"

" 'I Love L.A.' Know Randy Newman? Fuckin' incredible. He's famous, you know. Randy Newman... fuckin' incredible."

"Ever heard of the 'Offramp Slasher'? Dumps his victims next to freeway offramps, in the bushes... Hollywood?"

"Heard of what he did. I was at this topless bar. Saw it on the TV. He cuts off peoples'... (smiles)... cuts off everything, right?"

"How'd you know what he did? Wasn't ever printed in the paper. Wasn't on the news either. Only the killer would know that. How'd you know, Jimmy?"

Silence. Toying with a hole in greasy jeans, tearing it like a cut in skin.

"Let's talk about Debbie Salerno."

"I'm thirsty. You said I could have a Coke."

"Debbie Salerno was found next to the Vine Street offramp and she'd been sexually... torn apart. Blonde, fifteen years old."

The greasy jeans tore more, fat white threads taut. Snapping. Eyes closed. Thin veins puffing at the temples. Brown teeth grinning stupidly, diseased and soft.

"We talked about her yesterday. Remember Jimmy? You gouged her eyes out while you raped her. You remember doing that? Remember how it felt?"

Pulling on upper lip. Shrug.

"It was okay. Somethin' to do."

"So tell me more."

"How many you say I killed? Thousand?"

"You can do better than that. How many was it, Jimmy?"

"I'm gonna be famous. Like Jack the Ripper. Randy Newman."

"Seventy-three. You killed 'em all. How tall was Debbie?"

"Debbie who?"

"Salerno."

"Never heard of her."

"Don't fuck with me, Jimmy, I'm running out of patience. You confessing or jerking me off?"

"Okay.... She was five-three, five-two. I don't know. She was screamin'... what'd'm I supposed to do, measure her?"

"How'd you meet her?"

"You tell me."

"Alright, you sick fuck, I'll tell you... here's exactly how it went down: you were in your van, cruising Sunset and you were shooting garbage. Maybe a couple hundred in your arm. You were cranked and you got that little urge you get. And then you saw her. Her hood was up. Starting to remember yet? She needed help ... you pulled over. What'd you say to her, Jimmy?"

A big smile. Cracked lips stretching.

"I said, 'Hey... pretty lady... need a lift, or did you lose somethin' in there?' She thought that was funny. She got in and we drove."

"Where'd you do it, Jimmy?"

"Somewhere... lots of lights. A view."

"Hollywood hills? Above the strip?"

"I guess. Hey man, it's hot in here."

"Answer the question. Hollywood hills?"

"Okay, man! Hollywood hills! You happy? Get off my ass!"

"We're not done yet."

"*I'm* done! You're driving me fuckin' crazy with all your questions."

Biting skin off bottom lip. Tasting the blood.

"Tell me more."

"Whattya mean more? Whattya want... you wanna hear about all of 'em one more time?"

"Yeah."

"Like who?"

"Anybody you want. You got a big list, remember?"

"So whattya want? Guys? Fags? Kids?"

"Upset about something?"

"I know all this shit! I know how it went down! I know what it looked like and smelled like. I saw the faces... heard the begging. So fuck off!"

"I'm here to find out if you really did it, Jimmy. That's why we've been doing this for three weeks and you know it. You tired? So am I. So, you give me the details... we can get this over with and you're in a nice quiet cell."

"Fuck you, man! I answer no more. I know all this shit. I'm tired. I need sleep. We've been through this. I know every name, every offramp, what they were wearing, how they were found! How many pieces I cut 'em into. You can't mess with my head. I *know*. Now give me a fuckin' Coke! I want my fuckin' Coke!"

"How did you kill Thomas Dremmond?"

"Senior or junior? I killed 'em both, remember? Nice try. Told you about it day before yesterday."

Knuckles rubbed into bloodshot eyes.

"How'd you do it?"

"Fire. Torched him. Like I told you. I'm tired."

"How about Donald Belli?"

"Cut everything out."

"Which way was he facing?"

"Oh, fuck you! Toward Highland Ave, okay? We've been through this!"

"Maria Vera. How?"

"Coathanger. Body left sitting up. Get me a fuckin' Coke!"

"Not easy being famous is it?"

The man in the tie looked at him. Stared. Thought.

"Alright... I'm convinced. Get out."

The needled arm reached back and grabbed a torn duffel filled with bloody clothes. The rotted smile looked at the man with the tie.

"Tell them what you told me, you'll be famous. Keep it exact. Here's change for a drink."

The brown teeth grinned and the retarded young man with the duffel got out and walked toward the police station, mind bloated with hideous facts that were now memorized; now his.

The man in the tie watched him enter, then pulled away and drove on toward Texas, almost getting the urge when a Cadillac cut him off.

WHERE THERE'S A WILL

HE AWOKE.

It was dark and cold. Silent.

I'm thirsty, he thought. He yawned and sat up; fell back with a cry of pain. He'd hit his head on something. He rubbed at the pulsing tissue of his brow, feeling the ache spread back to his hairline.

Slowly, he began to sit up again but hit his head once more. He was jammed between the mattress and something overhead. He raised his hands to feel it. It was soft and pliable, its texture yielding beneath the push of his fingers. He felt along its surface. It extended as far as he could reach. He swallowed anxiously and shivered.

What in God's name was it?

He began to roll to his left and stopped with a gasp. The surface was blocking him there, as well. He reached to his right and his heart beat faster. It was on the other side, as well. He was surrounded on four sides. His heart compressed like a smashed soft drink can, the blood spurting a hundred times faster.

Within seconds, he sensed that he was dressed. He felt trousers, a coat, a shirt and tie, a belt. There were shoes on his feet.

He slid his right hand to his trouser pocket and reached in. He palmed a cold, metal square and pulled his hand from the pocket, bringing it to his face. Fingers trembling, he hinged the top open and spun the wheel with his thumb. A few sparks glinted but no flame. Another turn and it lit.

He looked down at the orange cast of his body and shivered again. In the light of the flame, he could see all around himself.

He wanted to scream at what he saw.

He was in a casket.

He dropped the lighter and the flame striped the air with a yellow tracer before going out. He was in total darkness, once more. He could see nothing. All he heard was his terrified breathing as it lurched forward, jumping from his throat.

How long had he been here? Minutes? Hours?

Days?

His hopes lunged at the possibility of a nightmare; that he was only dreaming, his sleeping mind caught in some kind of twisted vision. But he knew it wasn't so. He knew, horribly enough, exactly what had happened.

They had put him in the one place he was terrified of. The one place he had made the fatal mistake of speaking about to them. They couldn't have selected a better torture. Not if they'd thought about it for a hundred years.

God, did they loathe him that much? To do *this* to him?

He started shaking helplessly, then caught himself. He wouldn't let them do it. Take his life and his business all at once? No, goddamn them, *no*!

He searched hurriedly for the lighter. That was their mistake, he thought. Stupid bastards. They'd probably thought it was a final, fitting irony: A gold-engraved thank-you for making the corporation what it was. On the lighter were the words: *Charlie/ Where There's a Will...*

"Right" he muttered. He'd beat the lousy sons of bitches. They weren't going to murder him and steal the business he owned and built. There *was* a will.

His.

He closed his fingers around the lighter and, holding it with a white-knuckled fist, lifted it above the heaving of his chest. The wheel ground against the flint as he spun it back with his thumb. The flame caught and he quieted his breathing as he surveyed what space he had in the coffin.

Only inches on all four sides.

How much air could there be in so small a space he wondered? He clicked off the lighter. Don't burn it up, he told himself. Work in the dark.

Immediately, his hands shot up and he tried to push the lid up. He pressed as hard as he could, his forearms straining. The lid remained fixed. He closed both hands into tightly balled fists and pounded them against the lid until he was coated with perspiration, his hair moist.

He reached down to his left-trouser pocket and pulled out a chain with two keys attached. They had placed those with him, too. *Stupid bastards.* Did they really think he'd be so terrified he couldn't *think*? Another amusing joke on their part. A way to lock up his life completely. He wouldn't need the keys to his car and to the office again so why not put them in the casket with him?

Wrong, he thought. He *would* use them again.

Bringing the keys above his face, he began to pick at the lining with the sharp edge of one key. He tore through the threads and began to rip apart the lining. He pulled at it with his fingers until it popped free from its fastenings. Working quickly, he pulled at the downy stuffing, tugging it free and placing it at his sides. He tried not to breathe too hard. The air had to be preserved.

He flicked on the lighter and looking at the cleared area, above, knocked against it with the knuckles of his free hand. He sighed with relief. It was oak, not metal. Another mistake on their part. He smiled with contempt. It was easy to see why he had always been so far ahead of them.

"Stupid bastards," he muttered, as he stared at the thick wood. Gripping the keys together firmly, he began to dig their serrated edges against the oak. The flame of the lighter shook as he watched small pieces of the lid being chewed off by the gouging of the keys. Fragment after fragment fell. The lighter kept going out and he had to spin the flint over and over, repeating each move, until his hands felt numb. Fearing that he would use up the air, he turned the lighter off again, and continued to chisel at the wood, splinters of it falling on his neck and chin.

His arm began to ache.

He was losing strength. Wood no longer coming off as steadily. He laid the keys on his chest and flicked on the lighter again. He could see only a tattered path of wood where he had dug but it was only inches long. It's not enough, he thought. It's not enough.

He slumped and took a deep breath, stopping halfway through. The air was thinning. He reached up and pounded against the lid.

"Open this thing, goddammit," he shouted, the veins in his neck rising beneath the skin. "*Open this thing and let me out!*"

I'll die if I don't do something more, he thought.

They'll win.

His face began to tighten. He had never given up before. Never. And they weren't going to win. There was no way to stop him once he made up his mind.

He'd show those bastards what willpower was.

Quickly, he took the lighter in his right hand and turned the wheel several times. The flame rose like a streamer, fluttering back and forth before his eyes. Steadying his left arm with his right, he held the flame to the casket wood and began to scorch the ripped grain.

He breathed in short, shallow breaths, smelling the butane and wood odor as it filled the casket. The lid started to speckle with tiny sparks as he ran the flame along the gouge. He held it to one spot for several moments then slid it to another spot. The wood made faint crackling sounds.

Suddenly, a flame formed on the surface of the wood. He coughed as the burning oak began to produce gray pulpy smoke. The air in the casket continued to thin and he felt his lungs working harder. What air was available tasted like gummy smoke, as if he were lying in a horizontal smokestack. He felt as though he might faint and his body began to lose feeling.

Desperately, he struggled to remove his shirt, ripping several of the buttons off. He tore away part of the shirt and wrapped it around his right hand and wrist. A section of the lid was beginning to char and had become brittle. He slammed his swathed fist and forearm against the smoking wood and it crumbled down on him, glowing embers falling on his face and neck. His arms scrambled frantically to slap them out. Several burned his chest and palms and he cried out in pain.

Now a portion of the lid had become a glowing skeleton of wood, the heat radiating downward at his face. He squirmed away from it, turning his head to avoid the falling pieces of wood. The casket was filled with smoke and he could breathe only the choking, burning smell of it. He coughed, his throat hot and raw. Fine-powder ash filled his mouth and nose as he pounded at the lid with his wrapped fist. Come on, he thought. Come on.

"Come on!" he screamed.

The section of lid gave suddenly and fell around him. He slapped at his face, neck and chest but the hot particles sizzled on his skin and he had to bear the pain as he tried to smother them.

The embers began to darken, one by one, and now he smelled something new and strange. He searched for the lighter at his side, found it, and flicked it on.

He shuddered at what he saw.

Moist, root laden soil packed firmly overhead.

Reaching up, he ran his fingers across it. In the flickering light, he saw burrowing insects and whiteness of earthworms, dangling inches from his face. He drew down as far as he could, pulling his face from their wriggling movements.

Unexpectedly, one of the larva pulled free and dropped. It fell to his face and its jellylike casing stuck to his upper lip. His mind erupted with revulsion and he thrust both hands upward, digging at the soil. He shook his head wildly as the larva were thrown off. He continued to dig, the dirt falling in on him. It poured into his nose and he could barely breathe. It stuck to his lips and slipped into his mouth. He closed his eyes tightly but could feel it clumping on the lids. He held his breath as he pistoned his hands upward and forward like a maniacal digging machine. He eased his body up, a little at a time, letting the dirt collect under him. His lungs were laboring, hungry for air. He didn't dare open his eyes. His fingers became raw from digging, nails bent backward on several fingers, breaking off. He couldn't even feel the pain or the running blood but knew the dirt was being stained by its flow. The pain in his arms and lungs grew worse with each passing second until shearing agony filled his body. He continued to press himself upward, pulling his feet and knees closer to his chest. He began to wrestle himself into a kind of spasmed crouch, hands above his head, upper arms gathered around his face. He clawed fiercely at the dirt which gave way with each shoveling gouge of his fingers. Keep going, he told himself. *Keep going.* He refused to lose control. Refused to stop and die in the earth. He bit down hard, his teeth nearly breaking from the tension of his jaws. *Keep going*, he thought. *Keep going!* He pushed up harder and harder, dirt cascading over his body, gathering in his hair and on his shoulders. Filth surrounded him. His lungs felt ready to burst. It seemed like minutes since he'd taken a breath. He wanted to scream from his need for air but couldn't. His fingernails began to sting and throb, exposed cuticles and nerves rubbing against the granules of dirt. His mouth opened in pain and was filled with dirt, covering his tongue and gathering in his throat. His gag reflex jumped and he began retching, vomit and dirt mixing as it exploded from his mouth. His head began to empty of life as he felt himself breathing in more dirt, dying of asphyxiation. The clogging dirt began to fill his air passages, the beat of his heart doubled. *I'm losing!* he thought in anguish.

Suddenly, one finger thrust up through the crust of earth. Unthinkingly, he moved his hand like a trowel and drove it through to the surface. Now, his arms went crazy, pulling and punching at the dirt until an opening expanded. He kept thrashing at the opening, his entire system glutted with dirt. His chest felt as if it would tear down the middle.

Then his arms were poking themselves out of the grave and within several seconds he had managed to pull his upper body from the ground. He kept pulling, hooking his shredded fingers into the earth and sliding his legs from the hole. They yanked out and he lay on the ground completely, trying to fill his lungs with gulps of air. But no air could get through the dirt which had collected in his windpipe and mouth. He writhed on the ground, turning on his back and side until he'd finally raised himself to a forward kneel and began hacking phlegm-covered mud from his air passages. Black saliva ran down his chin as he continued to throw up violently, dirt falling from his mouth to the ground. When most of it was out he began to gasp, as oxygen rushed into his body, cool air filling his body with life.

I've *won*, he thought. I've beaten the bastards, *beaten* them! He began to laugh in victorious rage until his eyes pried open and he looked around, rubbing at his blood-covered lids. He heard the sound of traffic and blinding lights glared at him. They crisscrossed on his face, rushing at him from left and right. He winced, struck dumb by their glare, then realized where he was.

The cemetery by the highway.

Cars and trucks roared back and forth, tires humming. He breathed a sigh at being near life again; near movement and people. A grunting smile raised his lips.

Looking to his right, he saw a gas station sign high on a metal pole several hundred yards up the highway.

Struggling to his feet, he ran.

As he did, he made a plan. He would go to the station, wash up in the rest room, then borrow a dime and call for a limo from the company to come and get him. No. Better a cab. That way he could fool those sons of bitches. Catch them by surprise. They undoubtedly assumed he was long gone by now. Well, he had beat them. He knew it as he picked up the pace of his run. Nobody could stop you when you really wanted something, he told himself, glancing back in the direction of the grave he had just escaped.

He ran into the station from the back and made his way to the bathroom. He didn't want anyone to see his dirtied, bloodied state.

There was a pay phone in the bathroom and he locked the

door before plowing into his pocket for change. He found two pennies and a quarter and deposited the silver coin. They'd even provided him with money, he thought; the stupid bastards.

He dialed his wife.

She answered and screamed when he told her what had happened. She screamed and screamed. What a hideous joke she said. Whoever was doing this was making a hideous joke. She hung up before he could stop her. He dropped the phone and turned to face the bathroom mirror.

He couldn't even scream. He could only stare in silence.

Staring back at him was a face that was missing sections of flesh. Its skin was gray, and withered yellow bone showed through.

Then he remembered what else his wife had said and began to weep. His shock began to turn to hopeless fatalism.

It had been over seven months, she'd said.

Seven months.

He looked at himself in the mirror again, and realized there was nowhere he could go.

And somehow all he could think about was the engraving on his lighter.